Candita's Choice

Candita's Choice

MINA LEWITON

Pictures by Howard Simon

HARPER & ROW, PUBLISHERS

NEW YORK, EVANSTON, AND LONDON

Fic
Lew

*T*o Matilde Perez de Silva
affectionately

1

THINGS happened quickly after the letter.

One day Candita was in Mayagüez as always —going to school, walking along the beach, talking to Paquita—and the next day she was in San Juan standing beside the airplane.

"Do not be afraid," said Mama. "It is only an airplane." She held Candita's hand securely. "It is an ordinary airplane that is going to New York."

1

The plane, all the same, was surprising. If one saw a plane, it was high overhead and swift as wind. Long before it was seen, its vibrating noise was heard.

Today Candita stood beside the plane. It did not move, and it was silent. There it lay on the ground, a great silver fish shining in the sun.

Candita found herself not only standing beside the airplane, but walking into it, and sitting down beside Mama. More than that, in a matter of minutes, the plane rose from the ground and flew through clouds that were themselves flying, changing, appearing and disappearing.

But first came the letter. One morning when they were still at home in Mayagüez, Mama opened the envelope that Tonio Ramirez had brought, and read the letter.

"What do you say to this, Candita?" she said. "We shall soon see Papa and Margarita and Josef and Fernanda. And Martina and Josefina."

"Are they coming home at last?" With all her heart Candita hoped they were.

"We will go to them, Candita. To New York." Mama said this, her head tilted, as if astonished by her own words and as if, in any case, she did not truly believe what she was saying. "Look, here are the tickets. Papa has saved his money each week. Now he has bought these plane tickets."

Mrs. Rodriguez, who lived in the next street, happened to come in.

Mama told her, too, that they were leaving for New York. "José has a good job, that of transporting vegetables on a truck. He saves money each week. Look, here are the tickets he has bought with these savings."

"Well, then, that is how it will be," said Mrs. Rodriguez, nodding sagely.

Mrs. Rodriguez did not stay long. On her way to the market she told a great many people of José's good job, of the vegetables on the truck, and of the departure of Mrs. Rivera and Candita. "They are leaving tomorrow," she said. "I think we will prepare a little celebra-

3

tion for them this evening, no?" Mrs. Rodriguez sighed. It was impossible to know if she were sad or happy over this turn of events. Perhaps a little of each.

The word spread quickly. In the evening, all the nearby neighbors and even a few distant ones dropped in to hear how the Riveras had received the tickets for the airplane to New York, and to wish them a happy journey.

"I have worked in New York for one year," said Pedro Chavez, as soon as he entered the

house. "Everything is enclosed, the home, the factory. For myself, I would not live there. I prefer the open fields."

Everyone looked at Pedro in silence.

Juan Ardinez said, on the contrary, it was a fact that New York was a rare city. He added that if he, Juan, could save up enough for the plane, he and his wife and their four children would be glad to go there. Jobs were not scarce there and one could earn much money.

"My brother's son, Ramón, not yet eighteen years old, delivers the orders of a meat store in New York City. For this he receives twenty-five dollars a week. That is *money*," Juan said. "With this, one can buy many useful needed things. My brother's son has already bought a television set."

"But," said Pedro Chavez, "the cost of an apartment can also be twenty-five dollars a week. I say this because I know."

"I have heard," said Juan, "that one manages. There are others who will share this apartment and so reduce the cost. Look, if five share, the cost is five dollars only for each."

"It is the sharing that is bad," Pedro Chavez said quietly. "It is without dignity. It leads to quarrels and to lack of cleanliness. It benefits only the landlord. The landlord never receives so much rent as when many agree to share."

Again everyone looked in reproachful silence at Pedro.

"It is a celebration, Pedro," said Mrs. Ortíz reprovingly, and turned to Candita. "There are always those," she said, "who prefer to remain all their lives on the same foot of ground. As for me, I am for travel."

"I, too," her brother Manuel said. "And for having a job and buying a television set."

Candita's friend Paquita came running in. "I am sorry I am late. Are you leaving, Candita? Is it true? What shall I do without you?"

"Yes, it is true," Candita said, wondering if it *were* true.

It became crowded in the small house of the Riveras, yet it was good to have all their friends come at once.

"I will miss you, Rosita. There will be no one from whom to borrow this or that," Mrs.

Reyes said to Mama, laughing and crying at the same time.

"We will try to return one day," said Mama, "to see our old friends."

Mrs. Rodriguez nodded doubtfully.

"My daughter Margarita," said Mama to her, "now has two children I have not even seen."

"From the moment that you arrive in New York," said Basile Gomez, "you are in a city that is fantastic. I have heard from my cousin Alfonso about it. There are perhaps one million people living in New York City. One *million!*"

"I must correct you," said Pedro Chavez. "Eight million live there. I say this because I know."

"It is possible," said Basile. "My cousin Alfonso has not written me for two months."

Everyone had brought presents of food and packages of sweets. Mama unwrapped these and set them out on large and small plates.

"Please," said Mama, "please eat the *pas-*

teles. There is enough here for one hundred people. Here is the *arroz con dulce* I prepared this morning. Please come and eat. There is enough for all."

Mama turned on the electric bulb, decorated for tonight with leaves of the royal palm. The guests sat on chairs and benches and ate and talked, and ate more and talked more.

It was warm and the door was opened wide. A big yellow moon, low in the sky, looked in on them.

Antonio Mendez took up his guitar and began to sing.

> If I hadn't been born
> In the land where I was born
> I'd be sorry
> I hadn't been born there . . .

The guests, one by one, joined in the singing.

It was as beautiful as a birthday party or a wedding, Candita thought. Instead of saying good-by, their friends were singing good-by to them.

Antonio sang every song he could remember, and he could remember hundreds.

The last to arrive was Renaldo Montez. Renaldo lived far away. He shook hands with everyone before coming to sit beside Candita. He listened gravely to the singing and the lively conversation, yet he did not join the singers or the talkers.

Renaldo took from his pocket an orange scarf wrapped around a small bulky object and gave it to Candita. She laid it on the table with the other presents of sweets.

"It is for you, Candita," Renaldo said. "Look at it now if you like."

She untied the scarf. He had brought her a carving of a rabbit, polished and smooth. The rabbit was of wood, but it looked as agile as a live one. Its ears were laid back as if it were leaping over tall grass.

"It was completed only this evening, Candita."

"Thank you, Renaldo, thank you very much," she said, not finding the words to tell him how much she loved it.

"We shall miss seeing you, Renaldo, each Sunday afternoon," said Mama.

10

"It is a habit I formed," said Renaldo, "and it will be difficult to break." He stood up. "I must begin to walk home. Good-by, Rosita. Good-by, Candita." Renaldo took a long time to shake hands with them.

Candita said, "Good-by, Renaldo. Take this, that I have made, for the rabbit you have given me." She opened her hand. In it lay a little figure of clay, hardened by the hot sun.

He turned it about. "It is well made, Candita. I am happy to have it."

"It is many years now," said Mrs. Rodriguez after Renaldo left, "that he has lost his wife."

Mama sighed deeply.

Pedro said, "I have much sympathy for Renaldo. In the morning he is up before it is light. He works in the fields, without stopping, until the sun is high. Then only does he take the time for his own work, for his carvings and his pictures."

It was late when the last of their guests left.

Mama stayed up a little longer after Candita went to bed. She had washed Candita's red-flowered dress that afternoon, and now she

11

ironed it. At last she finished the ironing and turned off the light.

Candita lay in the darkness. After all the laughter and the conversation and the singing, it was now quiet. There was only the song of the little tree frogs in the soft warm silence. Through the window she could see a square of starry sky.

Tomorrow they would be in San Juan, she thought, and they would ride in a plane. She could scarcely believe it. Once before she had traveled to San Juan, a place of tree-lined paved streets and many people and stores.

It would be a long time before morning. The more she thought of San Juan and of the plane, the wider awake she became. Only she and Mama were leaving. Everyone else they knew would remain in Mayagüez. Paquita Reyes would stay here. And Pedro, who had already been in New York and found it too enclosed. "It is without dignity," he had said. What did that mean? Renaldo Montez would remain here, too. She would no longer go to meet him each Sunday and walk back with

12

him to their house. She would never part with
the little leaping rabbit he had brought her.
It would be like taking part of Mayagüez with
her and it would remind her of Renaldo, who
always spoke gently to her, as if she were still
very young.

Once she and Mama had visited Renaldo.
Large and small pictures and many carvings
crowded Renaldo's one-room house. That day
he had made a drawing of her. "Candita, now
you will always be here," Renaldo had said. In
the picture he had put a red flower in her hair.

The light of the moon found its way into
the room, making it bright as daytime. She
could see her dress waiting for her on the chair.
Mama had taken Candita's sneakers from the
shelf. "For traveling in an airplane, shoes are
necessary," Mama had said. Now the shoes,
too, stood waiting for her feet under the chair.

2

THE NEXT DAY Candita and Mama sat in the plane. In Candita's hand was Renaldo's polished carving wrapped in the orange scarf.

"It is an ordinary airplane. Do not be frightened, Candita." Mama sat on the edge of the seat.

14

Candita had not thought of being frightened. Perhaps Mama said it because she herself was frightened of being in a plane, even in an ordinary one, and of being so far above the ground. Candita thought that, more than anything, Mama was frightened of riding away from Mayagüez, where she had been born.

As if she were truly frightened of the airplane, Candita held Mama's hand. Because of this, Mama forgot her own fear, and patted Candita's hand often, and leaned back more comfortably.

Candita could hardly believe they were moving until she looked out. Below, through thin wind-borne mist, there were little shining mirrors, broken into thousands of fragments, catching the sun.

"It is the ocean," said the lady of the plane to Candita. "The Atlantic Ocean."

Candita hoped the flying would never end.

She hoped it would never end, and she hoped, too, it would end and there would be even more miraculous things to see.

Candita looked about her. There were many

15

others in this plane—children and their mothers and fathers, all from her own island of Puerto Rico. She heard their voices. The words they were saying were familiar to her, and their clothes and their faces, too. It was as if she were still in Mayagüez, as if inside this plane they were all friends.

Then she looked at the bright blue of the sky. Her eyes became more and more tired as she watched the racing clouds and the shining sea with the dazzling sunlight upon it.

She tried holding her eyes open with her fingers, but now everything was becoming a blur of sunshine, little mirrors, and movement.

Then, without wanting to, Candita fell asleep. She had hardly slept the night before, but now she slept soundly and as if she were at home in her bed.

In her long sound sleep, she heard Mama say, "Candita, we are arriving. Candita, you have slept more than three hours."

Candita opened her eyes.

The plane was no longer among the clouds. From her window she could see people walking about on level ground.

"It is New York," Mama said in a small voice. "Do not be afraid. It is only the airport of New York."

People were calling to each other and greeting each other. Some were already walking away from the plane carrying bags and bundles and suitcases.

Mama and Candita walked down from the plane.

The airport was altogether different from Mayagüez and from San Juan. There were few trees here and these few were thin-leafed. There were no flowers to be seen. A sharp cold wind blew and a pale sun was setting in the sky. Near by a tiny baby cried. The baby, too, saw it was a new, strange, cold place.

Candita looked at Mama. Mama, shivering with cold, said, "I am happy that we have arrived." But she did not look happy.

Candita continued to hold Mama's hand, and Candita's other hand held the wood carving inside the orange scarf.

They heard someone call, "Look, look, Rosita, Candita! Rosita—Candita, look, I am coming!"

It was Papa and he was hurrying toward them.

18

3

PAPA was surprising, too. He was wearing a brown leather jacket with a thick warm collar. Candita had seen such coats only in pictures of faraway cold places.

"Rosita, Candita, welcome to New York!" Papa said, trying to put one arm around both at once. On his other arm, Papa carried a pile of coats. "Margarita and Fernanda sent these for you to wear home. In this climate of the north, coats are necessary."

The pile of coats became only two coats. He put the heavy white one on Mama and the soft thick pink one on Candita. Both coats were too large, but it was better to be warm inside too-large coats than to shiver.

"They are all waiting for you," said Papa. "Candita, you have grown twice as tall as when I saw you last. How do you both feel? How was this airplane?"

"We are both feeling well, José. But it was too much," said Mama, shaking her head and trying to laugh. "I am not used to airplanes. I am glad we are again on the ground. Candita fell asleep. For me sleep was not possible. I was a little frightened, José, I must confess. I like a quieter place than an airplane."

"Yes," said Papa, "but in a little while you will not mind all this, Rosita. There are not too many quiet places in New York. Everything is different from Mayagüez. Everything is large—buildings, crowds, streets."

"It is always so cold, too?"

20

"It has been much, much colder than this," said Papa.

"It is cold enough for me." Mama held the white coat closely about her.

"It is now April, the season of spring," said Papa. "Soon it will be warmer. You will see."

As Papa said, everything was large. He took them home in a large bus, then in a train of many cars, lighted by many electric lights. The train moved as fast as the plane, Candita thought, and made even more noise.

"It is nothing, Candita," Papa said. "It is only the subway."

When they came to Papa's house, they entered by a narrow door. This house and all the others near by were tall as mountains. They climbed up and up. There were five sets of steep stairs to climb. At the end of their climb they found themselves in darkness.

"Again the light has failed on our floor," said Papa. "Usually one can see one's way."

Papa felt his way to the door.

The moment it was opened a crowd surrounded them. "Candita, Mama, welcome!"

21

Fernanda, Margarita, Margarita's husband, Josef, and their two little girls, Martina, two, and Josefina, three, were calling out, "Mama, Candita, Mama, Candita, welcome home!"

"It is our own family," Mama said. "We see our family at last!"

Inside it was brightly lighted. The electric bulbs were under shades of red and green and yellow. Ribbons of pink and blue crepe paper were looped from the ceiling across the room to each corner. On the square table there was a pink-flowered paper tablecloth and napkins of the same design. A vase was filled with red and white paper carnations.

Margarita and the little girls and their father and Fernanda, one after the other, threw their arms around Mama and Candita.

"Candita, you are more beautiful than I remember," said Margarita.

Fernanda, younger than Margarita, was the gayest and liveliest of all. "Much, much more!" She put her arms around Candita and danced her in and out among the furniture and around the table. "Welcome, Candita, this house is

now yours, too. And at last Mama is here with us. How we have missed you!"

"At last," said Mama, putting her arms around each, "we are all together!"

They drank papaya juice poured into paper cups from large cans. They offered each other sliced pineapple and coconut cookies, peppermints and chocolates.

They did not stop urging Mama and Candita to eat and drink. "Have this—and this, too, and this—"

It was again like looking out of the plane upon the shining water. The paper ribbons and the flowers, the lively conversation, the two little girls hopping up and down in their bright red dresses, the bowls full of striped candies, the fruit, the peanuts, the papaya juice, and the cookies began to blur and run into each other as Candita looked around, and Candita herself felt as if she were swaying from one side of the room to the other.

"Candita is tired," she heard Mama say at last. "And I, too, am tired. Do not forget, from now on we shall always be together."

Although she was half-asleep, Candita saw that the room was changing. Beds appeared from somewhere, pillows and quilts were brought out.

She was almost asleep and not yet in bed. It seemed to her for a moment she was back in Puerto Rico listening to the music of Antonio's guitar.

She heard Margarita say this strange thing:

24

"The guitar you hear, Mama, is played by Mr. Calles. He plays on the radio for *La Paloma* spaghetti. We are fortunate to have him as a neighbor."

As Candita was getting into bed, Papa said, "Tomorrow I will take Candita to her new school."

With her head on the pillow she imagined the new school. She saw it clearly, but it was not the new school after all. It was the little school of Mayagüez and beside the door was the *flamboyán* tree covered with its bright blue blossoms, and hurrying through the door was Paquita, late as always.

Candita was asleep.

4

CANDITA opened her eyes. Nothing looked familiar. Pink and blue crepe paper decorated the ceiling. Then she remembered the airplane. And the subway. And the new family. This is my new house, she thought. I am in New York.

The flowers and the chocolates and the striped candies had disappeared. The two little girls, in white dresses, were playing on a blanket on the floor.

It was Papa's voice: "When I have brought Candita to school, I can go to work. Then Margarita will take you, Rosita, and the little ones, also, to see the school, and to get Candita at the hour of lunch. The time to be at the school is twelve o'clock. As soon as Candita awakes we will go to the school."

Candita sat up. "I am awake," she said.

All the tiredness was gone. She was anxious to see the new school.

Last night, although she had been half-asleep, she had asked Papa to set Renaldo's rabbit on a shelf. There it was, looking down at her. It now seemed an old friend who had come along from Mayagüez.

Candita put on her dress with the design of red flowers, and put on her sneakers. Mama combed Candita's hair smoothly flat, and as they were leaving, Margarita slipped over Candita's shoulders the pink coat that belonged to Fernanda.

27

"You must wear this coat," Margarita said, opening the window and looking out on the street below. "Everyone is wearing a warm coat today. It is winter once more." Margarita looked at Candita. "It is true this coat is a little large for you." She turned back the cuffs once, and a second time, and Candita's hands were seen again.

Papa and Candita walked downstairs and toward a wide street into which they turned.

"It is Broadway," said Papa. "That is the name of this street."

On either side, the store windows were brimming with color and crowded with remarkable things. Ladies in flower-splashed summer dresses stood stiffly in one window. Candita stared.

"These ladies are artificial ones," said Papa.

Another store window was heaped high with vegetables and green bananas in huge bunches. Dainty high-heeled shoes were arranged in rows in another window, and in still another there were big and little lamps, brightly lighted even though it was daytime.

Candita could not understand a word of what people said to each other as they passed. These people looked different from the people of Mayagüez. They wore dark, more severe clothing. The children, too, did not look or speak like the children of Mayagüez.

"Are they speaking English?"

"It is English. And in a short time you will speak as well as I speak. Even better, perhaps," said Papa modestly. "The school will teach you. You have never seen such a school as the one we are going to."

When they turned the corner they saw it. It was a new school, made, it seemed to Candita, entirely of glass.

The glass doors were as tall as those of a cathedral. Candita and Papa walked through them and came into a sunlit hall. They seated themselves on a bench.

Almost at once, from behind closed doors, they heard an orchestra begin to play. A parade of children of all sizes came walking in pairs down the hall, passing Papa and Candita.

Candita had never seen so many children.

29

The youngest was no larger than Josefina, and the oldest was taller than she was. They looked curiously at her as they passed, and some whispered and laughed.

It was because of her too-large pink coat, she thought. She slipped out of it and put it on the bench beside Papa.

"This school," whispered Papa, "is not too much like the school of Mayagüez."

"No," she whispered back, "it is not too much like my old school."

The children all disappeared through another set of doors.

Papa said, "We shall have to ask how one begins to go to this school." But he continued to sit beside her in the lonely hall.

A door opened and a tall lady came toward them.

"Excuse me," said Papa, "is it possible for Candita to become a pupil of this school? If so, I will give you the information."

Candita was proud of Papa for speaking English so well. Although she did not understand a word of what he said, the lady of the school did.

"How do you do, Candita," she said in Spanish. To Papa she said, "It does not matter that Candita does not speak English. That is, in fact, a good reason for coming to school. Come into my office, please."

Papa answered all the questions. When there were no more questions to answer, he said good-by. To Candita, pressing her hand as if he were leaving to go on a long journey, Papa said softly, "I leave you now. In this

31

school it is necessary to listen carefully." After he had gone a few steps, Papa came back. "And to try to learn English."

The lady of the school took Candita upstairs. Together they went into a classroom.

Four boys and two girls were writing at a table. They stopped writing and stared at Candita.

"This is Miss Singer," the first lady of the school told Candita. "She is your teacher."

To Miss Singer, seated at her desk and facing the children, she said, "This is Candita."

"I am very glad to meet you, Candita." Miss Singer, too, spoke Spanish.

Candita looked long at Miss Singer. Miss Singer's hair was short, and golden as sunlight, and her eyes were the color of the sea. The most beautiful of all were Miss Singer's eyeglasses, which had tiny diamonds around their rims.

Miss Singer said, "Candita, please sit in the chair beside Alvaro. Alvaro, raise your hand."

The boy next to Alvaro raised Alvaro's hand for him.

When Candita had been sitting for a while in the chair beside Alvaro, Miss Singer came to her and said to her alone, and in a low voice, "We are going to be good friends, Candita."

Candita looked up at Miss Singer's beautiful smiling face and could not think of what to say. She nodded instead, rapidly, happily.

"Candita," Miss Singer said, going to the front of the room once more, "as you are going to be in this class from now on, we will explain what we do here. We read and write and learn a little more English each day. For today, Candita, see what the others do. That is enough for this day which is your first."

Miss Singer spoke slow and careful Spanish as if she, Miss Singer, were a little girl in a Mayagüez school beginning to read out of a Spanish book.

"Now, Candita, I will present you to Linda and to Carmen. And to Rafael and Barnabe and Alvaro and Luis."

As soon as possible, she would tell Miss Singer about the little school of Mayagüez and about the mango trees of Mayagüez. She would tell her about the edge of the beach and the color of the ocean and the stars of the Puerto Rican night that sparkled like the diamonds of Miss Singer's eyeglasses. She would tell Miss Singer everything.

Miss Singer spoke in English to her class of seven that now included Candita Rivera.

Then Miss Singer said, "Candita, I have just asked the others if they like to come to school. Do you hear what they say, Candita?"

"Yes, Miss Singer," the class chanted together.

Candita nodded.

"Say it, too, Candita."

Candita nodded once more. "Yes, yes," she repeated in a whisper to herself. "Yes, Miss Singer."

Miss Singer walked to a closet and brought back a book for Candita.

"Now, let us open our books," said Miss Singer. "Linda, please begin. Page 9."

Candita, seeing the others open their books, opened hers. There was a picture on each page and there were many words under each picture.

She looked intently at the words as if she could truly understand them.

Rafael leaned forward. He showed her the line Linda was reading aloud. She studied the line and tried to follow Linda, but it was as if she were trying to catch running water.

"Not so fast, Linda," said Miss Singer.

Linda came to the end of the page and turned it. Candita turned the page, too. On the next page there was a picture of a squirrel. Miss Singer talked about the squirrel.

Asquirrel. Candita repeated the sound to herself. It was a little like a Spanish word. *Asquirrel, asquirrel.* If Miss Singer would ask her, she could say this new word, too, but when Miss Singer told the class to say the new word aloud, Candita only whispered it again.

All morning she hoped Miss Singer would come and sit beside her as she had done for a little while with Alvaro. She could then begin to describe to Miss Singer a few of the things of Mayagüez.

Almost at the end of the morning, Miss Singer did come to sit beside her.

"Candita," Miss Singer said, drawing a chair up, "you will never learn English if I speak to you in Spanish. That is why I must speak English to you. Try to answer in English, too. It doesn't matter if you do not speak perfectly at first."

Candita nodded.

"At first I will try to speak more slowly to you than to the others. We will begin at once. From now on we speak English. That is the way to learn English quickly, Candita."

Miss Singer had said they were going to be good friends. But how could she speak to her friend in a language she, Candita, did not know?

"I will speak very slowly," Miss Singer repeated, but it was as if she were saying, *You must not talk to me, Candita, not unless you speak English.* It would be a long time before she would learn enough English to talk to Miss Singer, she thought.

Candita looked away from Miss Singer and down at her desk, giving all her attention to listening, as Papa had said. She tried very hard to listen to each word and to understand. She tried so hard, her ears ached with trying. It was no use. She did not begin to understand.

How had it happened? A little while ago everything had seemed right and good. Now everything was changed. How can I ever learn English quickly? she thought. How can I *begin* to learn?

The children, one after the other, read from the book. Candita looked out of the window at the cool blue sky. She was alone in a strange,

new, cold land where people talked an unknown language. At this moment in Mayagüez
the sun was hot and the air warm and the trees
and bushes bright with flowers. The beach
was wide and the waves made a soft crashing
sound.

She could see it as if she were truly there.
She and Paquita Reyes used to play all day and
talk. That had been the best of all, the talks
with Paquita while Paquita watched her make
little figures out of damp sand and clay.

In the hall a gong rang loud and deep. Its
echoing sound hung in the air.

Everyone in the classroom began to talk.

Linda leaned toward her. "Now we can
talk Spanish. Where did you come from?
What day was it when you arrived? Was it
raining? When I came it rained. We were wet
and we were cold."

"I came from Mayagüez," Candita said,
"the neighborhood of Buena Vista."

"And I, too, but from the neighborhood of
Dulces Lavios."

It was like home. Listening to Linda was like
Mayagüez and like home.

"Sit with me," the girl named Carmen said. "Eat your lunch here beside me, Linda. We can all sit together. You, too, Candita. I have been in this class two months."

"And I four months," said Barnabe. "When I came I could not speak. I was like you."

"She is a little shy," said Carmen. "You were not so shy."

"She is a shy one, you are right," said Barnabe, laughing again.

"Where are you going, Candita?" Linda asked. "All of us stay in school for our lunch."

Candita shook her head. Mama and Margarita and the children would be waiting for her as they had agreed. She hurried downstairs.

Instead of Margarita and Mama and the children, Fernanda had come.

"There was not enough work for a whole day in the factory so I came to walk home with you. Margarita has taken the little ones to the park." Fernanda put her arm around Candita's shoulders. "Well, how is this school?"

"They speak English."

"It is strange," said Fernanda, "when one does not understand, no?"

"Yes," said Candita, "it is strange."

"I went to school for a few evenings but I could not learn. It was as if the English words escaped from me. I have no ear for words. But children learn quickly," Fernanda said, looking anxiously at Candita. "Do not worry."

The English words escape from me, also, Candita thought. I, too, am one of those who have no ear for words. Fernanda knew how strange it was not to understand, but Fernanda did not have to go to school. Fernanda did not know that one was all alone in a classroom when one could not understand.

Perhaps Mama will feel as I do, she thought. Mama had already found it too cold here. She will want to return, too. Then we will all go back to Mayagüez. I hope so. I truly hope so.

She did not say this to Fernanda. Perhaps, when they reached the apartment, Mama would say it herself. Perhaps she would say it today. Candita began to walk more quickly.

But Mama did not talk of returning home.

5

THEY had been reading about the squirrel all week.

"Rafael," said Miss Singer, "what is the squirrel's name?"

"Bushy," said Rafael promptly, standing up.

"His whole name," said Miss Singer. "What is the squirrel's whole name? Like your whole name. Your whole name is Rafael Muñoz, isn't it?"

"That is my name," said Rafael. "And the squirrel's name is Bushy."

Alvaro raised his hand.

"Tell us, Alvaro," said Miss Singer.

"Bushy Tail," said Alvaro.

"That is right," said Miss Singer. "Very good, Alvaro." She turned to Candita and said slowly, "You see, Candita, Alvaro came only a few weeks before you to this class. Already he understands what we are saying. Alvaro learns quickly."

Candita looked at Alvaro. It seemed to her he had not understood either.

"Alvaro," said Miss Singer, "tell us how you came to New York."

Alvaro stood up and smiled but did not answer. He shook his head and lightly shrugged his shoulders.

"Alvaro, did you come from San Juan?"

"San Juan," repeated Alvaro.

"Where is San Juan?"

Alvaro looked over his shoulder.

"In Puerto Rico?" asked Miss Singer.

"Yes," said Alvaro. "Puerto Rico."

42

"How did you come?" said Miss Singer.

"I come here," said Alvaro.

"How?" said Miss Singer. "Did you walk?" Miss Singer walked the forefinger of each hand on her desk.

"Yes," said Alvaro, wishing to be agreeable. He smiled at the walking fingers.

All the children laughed. Alvaro laughed, too.

"On the water? You walked across the water from San Juan to New York?" asked Miss Singer, raising her eyebrows.

Candita held her breath and listened to each word. Why were they laughing? She, too, would say *Yes* to every one of Miss Singer's questions. The children would laugh at her just as they were laughing at Alvaro.

Alvaro was brave. She would not laugh, Candita thought. More likely she would cry. Yes, she would surely cry. She was very sorry for Alvaro.

Miss Singer began all over again. "Alvaro, did you come from San Juan to New York?"

"Yes," said Alvaro, still smiling.

"Did you come on a plane to New York?"

"Ah, yes," said Alvaro, understanding at last. "Plane." .

"In a plane. You did not walk on the water."

"Ah, no," said Alvaro.

The children could not stop laughing.

Miss Singer held up her hand for silence and said to Alvaro, "Was it a big plane?"

"Big," said Alvaro.

"Yes," said Miss Singer patiently, "in a big plane. Sit down, Alvaro."

Alvaro dropped into his seat and drew a deep breath.

Miss Singer wrote in a book.

In the little silence, Candita made up her mind: she would not say a single word. She would listen and say nothing. Even when she understood Miss Singer's question and knew the answer, too. Only when she could talk like Miss Singer would she talk in school. Not a day before then. Not in English. Only if Miss Singer talked to her in Spanish would she answer her.

She would not talk like a small child. She

would not say *big, plane, yes, no*. She would speak English when she could talk about the shining ocean and the skimming clouds and the airport and the baby crying because it was a strange, new, cold land.

She would wait. She would wait until she could talk well enough so they would all say, *Candita speaks well. She understands and speaks English very well. Was Candita born in New York?* She would wait until someone could say, *It seems to me Candita speaks as if she were born in New York. . . .*

6

"COME HERE, Candita," said Miss Singer. "Help me with these crayons, please."

Candita sat still. *Come here* were words she knew, but now she looked away from Miss Singer.

In her slow, careful, childish Spanish, Miss Singer said, "Come here, Candita. Stand beside my desk."

Candita stood up and came to Miss Singer's desk.

In Spanish, Candita said, "Here I am."

Miss Singer looked disappointed.

"Now, girls and boys," said Miss Singer turning to the others, "take three crayons each from Candita. Candita will come to you with the crayon box. Help yourselves from the box." She gave Candita a flat wide box full of crayons of all colors. "After you have chosen your crayons draw something that you saw yesterday. What day was yesterday, Luis?"

"Yesterday it was Sunday," said Luis, standing up and speaking in a loud voice.

"Yes, yesterday was Sunday. Where did you go, Luis?"

"I go to the zoo," said Luis.

"I *went* to the zoo," said Miss Singer.

"You, too?" said Luis, pointing at Miss Singer.

Everyone except Alvaro and Candita laughed.

"No, I did not go," said Miss Singer, "but you must say, 'I *went* to the zoo.' "

"O.K.," said Luis. "I went to the zoo."

"Did you understand, Candita?"

Candita said nothing.

Miss Singer said in Spanish, "Please go from

one to another so they may choose the crayons. Then do as the others do, Candita. Draw a picture."

Candita went with the crayons from one to the other. When everyone had taken crayons out of the box, Candita chose for herself a blue, a red, and a yellow. They were new and bright in color and smelled pleasantly of wax in the warm room. Then she went to her own chair.

Alvaro had begun to draw rapidly. Candita watched him. He, too, had been recently at the zoo, Candita thought, for he was drawing a giraffe. She knew what the zoo was and what a giraffe was because Papa had taken her and Margarita's little girls to the zoo. They had all seen the giraffe the first Sunday Candita had been in New York.

Candita began to draw on her paper. Blue for the sky with white uneven spaces left for clouds. Among the clouds Candita drew an airplane. Beneath all of it she drew a dark blue sea.

When she had finished, she saw that Rafael

was looking at her picture. He said in Spanish to her, "This is a good picture."

"It is a scene I remember," said Candita.

"I, too," said Rafael. "The picture you have made recalls it to me."

Candita said, "Far below our plane were a thousand little mirrors."

"I remember that also," said Rafael.

Miss Singer said, "Remember, we speak English in the classroom. Are you speaking English, Rafael?"

"She does not yet understand English," said Rafael.

Miss Singer shook her head slowly at Rafael.

Candita went on drawing. She put some tiny patches of yellow over the blue of the sea and these places began to look like sunlight on water. More and more it seemed to her to resemble the ocean she had flown over. She did not speak to Rafael. Rafael spoke, instead, to Barnabe and to Linda in English.

On another sheet Candita began to draw a dog, asleep, forelegs stretched out.

Miss Singer walked by and stopped to watch

her drawing. She said, "We have clay, too, Candita."

Candita did not answer but she stopped drawing. Miss Singer went to the cupboard and took from it a box of green clay.

"Do you know what to do with this, Candita?"

Candita glanced at the box and almost forgot she had decided not to answer Miss Singer in English. "Yes, yes," she wanted to say. There were pictures of clay animals on the box cover. She knew at once what the clay was for. The clay was like the wet sand of Mayagüez beach but much, much better.

She modeled the sleeping dog out of the clay, giving him a mild, peaceful expression. Then she made a squirrel, looking watchful. She would have made many more animals but these two had used up the whole box of clay.

"Everyone can see them here," Miss Singer said, putting Candita's animals on the window sill, each beside a white-potted geranium.

It seemed to Candita that the whole room looked friendlier now that her animals were on the window sill.

7

CANDITA had been in Miss Singer's class for four weeks. It was the end of May and it was at last truly spring. It was almost as warm as the weather of Mayagüez in the month of Christmas.

At first all the words she heard had been new

and strange. Now, without knowing how it happened, Candita understood *O.K.* and *Hello* and *Good morning* and *Yes, Miss Singer* and *Good-by*. She knew *a squirrel* from seeing the picture in the book. But when Miss Singer talked to her, Candita looked down at her desk.

Miss Singer no longer urged Candita to answer her questions in English. She spoke patiently and slowly to Candita in Spanish and, in Spanish, Candita answered briefly.

One afternoon Mrs. Peterson came into the classroom. Mrs. Peterson was the first person Candita had seen in this school, the tall lady to whom Papa had given the information.

Mrs. Peterson walked around the room and looked at the drawings hung up by Miss Singer. She liked the work of Rafael, she said, and also that of Linda. Then she walked to the window sill and examined Candita's clay animals.

Mrs. Peterson spoke to Miss Singer and nodded. Candita heard Miss Singer say, "They were made by Candita Rivera."

Mrs. Peterson turned around and recognized Candita at once. She said in English, "I like your little animals, Candita. I wish I could have one for my office."

Candita wanted to say in English, "I will make you one." She almost did, but as she was about to say it, Miss Singer took Mrs. Peterson's arm and walked with her to the back of the room. Miss Singer talked to Mrs. Peterson in a low voice.

When the bell rang at noon, Linda came to sit beside Candita, who now stayed in school for lunch.

"You are too shy," said Linda at once. "Not only I think so. Miss Singer, too, thinks so. She told it to the principal. You do not have to be shy, Candita. Miss Singer understands that everyone makes mistakes. I made many in the beginning. I do not make so many now, but I still make a few."

"In the beginning, did the others laugh at you?"

Linda shrugged. "I did not want them to think I could not learn—that I am stupid."

She glanced quickly at Candita. "You are too shy. It is nothing else. And too silent. Candita, I will tell you something. Sometimes when one is shy it is the same as being stupid. I do not mean it is the same, but there are those who think that."

Linda had overheard Miss Singer speaking to Mrs. Peterson. Candita felt her face grow hot. "Miss Singer thinks I am stupid."

"She did not say that."

"I believe she said that."

"No. She said to Mrs. Peterson, 'Candita is a little slow.' "

"It is the same thing."

"No, not for me. For me it is the same as saying you are shy."

How could she tell Linda she wanted to say each English word right? She wanted to speak better even than Linda, who said she still made mistakes. No matter what Miss Singer thought, Candita would have to wait until she was sure all the words she said were right.

Linda said, "Look, Candita. We are both

eleven. Alvaro is thirteen and Rafael is fourteen and Luis is fourteen, too. They will soon go to other classes. If you will try, we, too, can soon leave Miss Singer. This class is only the preparation for the true class where we belong according to our age. But you must try, Candita."

Leave Miss Singer? Even if Miss Singer did not speak to her at all, and even if Miss Singer thought she was both slow and stupid instead of shy, she did not want to leave Miss Singer. It was enough to stay in her classroom and read a little in the book about Bushy Tail and make clay animals.

Candita at last began to eat her sandwich.

As usual, everyone had a meat sandwich for lunch. Almost everyone had a banana besides. Barnabe alone had a mango.

"If I had a knife," Barnabe said, "I would share this mango. But as I do not, I must eat it alone."

"We have mangoes at home," said Rafael. "I can wait. But I will take one small bite from yours, if you care to offer it to me."

Barnabe offered the ripe mango to Rafael, who took a small bite.

"Thank you very much," said Rafael.

Barnabe offered it to Candita, who refused.

Miss Singer came to their table. "May I join you?"

"You are very welcome, Miss Singer," said Barnabe.

"You would not care to have a bite of this mango of Barnabe's?" Rafael asked her.

"No, thank you, Rafael. Also, it is best to offer only what is your own. Thank you, Barnabe, for allowing me to join you at lunch," Miss Singer said. Then she turned to Candita and said slowly in English, "Can you hear all the mistakes I make when I speak Spanish, Candita?"

Candita understood each word. She wanted to say, No, you do not make many. Instead she smiled as Alvaro had done when Miss Singer had asked him about the plane.

"I know it takes a long time to speak English," said Miss Singer. "Some learn more quickly, others more slowly. With patience, everyone can learn."

After Miss Singer went to her desk, Linda said, "You cannot help it, Candita, if you are shy. As for me, I am not shy. If I were, my four sisters would get everything first and leave nothing for me."

"I have two sisters and two brothers," said Luis, "all smaller than I am. I am the oldest."

"You are an old man," said Barnabe.

Luis staggered around the room imitating an old man leaning on an imaginary cane. Everyone laughed at Luis.

"Please let us play some records, Miss Singer," Rafael said.

Miss Singer let them have the record player.

The music began. It brought back to Candita the memory of Mayagüez and the evenings when Antonio played his guitar. Listening to *Siboney* and thinking of Mayagüez, Candita longed to return there. But before she returned, she wanted Miss Singer to know she was not slow or stupid. Now, as she stood listening to the familiar music, Candita thought of a way to prove to Miss Singer she was not stupid:

She would learn the whole story of Bushy Tail. Word for word. Each day she would listen to the others, especially to Barnabe, who said it best. She could read all the words already, but her ears told her she did not say them yet as well as Barnabe. When she had learned the whole story well, she would say it for Miss Singer.

8

THIS afternoon Linda did not stop to talk with Candita after school.

"I must buy some things for supper," Linda said, "and I must prepare everything. My mother works overtime tonight. I will cook for the whole family. There are nine people in our house. Do you know I can cook *arroz con pollo?* I must cut up the onions, and the garlic,

and the pimientos, and I must add the toma-
toes, and add so much this, and so much that.
All this after my mother has already prepared
the chicken!" Linda laughed. "*Adios*, Candita." She waved and hurried away.

If Candita could not cook, at least she could
set the table. As soon as she arrived home, she
brought out plates and found pink paper napkins and folded them into triangles. Miss
Singer did that when she gave extra napkins to
those that needed them at lunch.

She glanced at the clock. Setting the table
had taken five minutes. The big hand would
have to go around the clock twice before anyone would be home and three times before
Papa and Josef would come. During these
sunny June days Margarita kept her little girls
in the park until the light went out of the sky.
Mama went to the factory each day with Fernanda. They came home together at five. Papa
and Josef had the longest hours. They came
home from the vegetable market long after six
o'clock.

Candita sat at the window. She read
through the story of Bushy Tail from begin-

60

ning to end. Then she leaned out of the window.

In Mayagüez at this season it would be too hot to do anything but run in and out of the ocean or walk at the edge of the water. She and Paquita, searching for shells, would keep their feet cool in the firm wet sand, and then look back at their footprints.

Candita watched two boys catching and throwing a ball far below in the street.

Yesterday, Mrs. Lopez, who lived on the floor below, had come to borrow a cup of rice. Mrs. Lopez had stayed and talked. It made the afternoon seem shorter. She wished someone else would come to borrow something—perhaps someone from the neighborhood of Buena Vista. Mrs. Lopez was from Ponce.

She continued to look out of the window and to listen to the boys' voices floating up to her.

There was a light quick rapping at the door.

"It is I," a high thin voice like a child's called out. "It is your neighbor, Mrs. Torres."

Candita ran to the door. It was as if Mrs. Torres had come in answer to her wish.

61

"I see your mother is not yet home," said Mrs. Torres, speaking rapidly, and looking around Candita on either side. Mrs. Torres was not much taller than Candita.

"No, not yet. She comes at five. Do you want to wait?"

"It does not matter, as it is you, anyway, I prefer to talk to, as I have a little favor to ask of you—and as I work in the factory and always to this very day my mother has remained at home and Jorge when he comes home from school finds her at home, all has been well, but it has happened today that my mother has entered the hospital, as she is not feeling well —no, I regret to say, she is not at all well—and so you can understand from this that I would like someone to help me—for as I am alone, what can I do? And what can my mother do?"

Candita tried to think how she could help Mrs. Torres or her mother, who was in the hospital.

"Come in, please," Candita said.

Mrs. Torres came in.

Mrs. Torres spoke even more rapidly inside

the house than at the door. "Between the hours when school is over and I return home, some-one must watch Jorge, for I can only continue to work if someone helps me to take care of him, otherwise I cannot work, for when Jorge is alone after school, he plays in the street and you do not know how I worry about Jorge, for the boys he plays with are older and stronger than he is and he is small—I do not mean he is small for his age, but I mean he is not so large as the largest of the boys and they may fight with him. Or he may get lost. A thousand things are possible without someone to take care of Jorge. I will tell you, Candita—your mother has already told me your name is Can-dita—my name is also Candita, that is to say, my name is Candelaria Rosas de Torres, but I am like you and my name is shortened a little so I am called Candita also, and as you can guess I am also from Mayagüez, as Candelaria is our blessed saint for whom I am named and you also—"

"You are from Mayagüez?"

"Yes, yes," Mrs. Torres continued, "from

the neighborhood of Poma Rosas. Now and then I receive letters from Mayagüez. If there is news, I will tell you at once, but I have not had a letter, as my sister is lazy and does not write too much, but the very next time she writes I will read her letter to you—"

"I would like that very much," Candita said. "We are from the neighborhood of Buena Vista. How old is Jorge, Mrs. Torres?"

"Jorge will be seven years old the day after tomorrow. I must tell you at once he is a very good boy. He is respectful and he obeys all adults. You will see for yourself," said Mrs. Torres. She went to the door, opened it wide, and called, "Jorge, come in here!"

His mother's voice rang through the hall.

Jorge burst out of a nearby door.

"Jorge, here is Candita, who will take care of you after school. But only if you are good, and she will wait for you since you are in the same school."

Candita was surprised.

Jorge looked happily from one to the other. Jorge's face was streaked with chocolate.

"It will be only for a few hours each day," said Mrs. Torres. "I leave the factory at four or a little later and I am at home at five or a little later and thank you one thousand times," said Mrs. Torres, "and remember that for you, too, it is a good thing, Candita, for you will no longer feel lonely coming home from school, as there will always be Jorge from now on—"

Candita had never felt lonely on the way home, but it would be well to see that Jorge reached home safely.

"And, also," added Mrs. Torres, "you can learn English by talking to Jorge. As you have only recently arrived in New York, Jorge will help you—he speaks perfect English. Speak English, Jorge."

Jorge said, "I speak O.K. English, I speak O.K. Spanish."

"You hear, Candita?" said his mother. "You hear how he speaks perfectly?"

Jorge took a walk around the room. "What is this?" he said reaching for a red paper flower in a vase. "Can I have it? I can bring it to my teacher."

65

His mother said, "Jorge likes his teacher.
The teacher invites me to come to see her but
there is no time."

"Yes," said Candita to Jorge, "take it."

Jorge climbed up on a chair to see what was
on the shelf. "What is in these boxes?" said
Jorge, lifting the top of one. "What is this?"
He picked up Renaldo's wood carving. "This
rabbit is O.K."

"Everybody likes Jorge," said his mother. "When he was only a baby everybody said, 'There is one who will be well liked.' Why? Because he is always happy and never cries. And it is true. From the time he was born he has always been happy."

Mrs. Torres told Candita not only what her mother and her father had remarked about Jorge when he was a few weeks old but also about her mother's present sickness and the sicknesses that she herself had suffered from and about her work at the factory, where she sewed dresses for children on a machine that was so noisy and so fast it frightened one, but only until one became accustomed to it . . .

When Margarita came home with the little girls, Mrs. Torres stayed on and told Margarita about her sick mother and the noisy machine. Then when Fernanda came home, Mrs. Torres told it all over again.

Mrs. Torres said, "Soon we are going home and Jorge will go to sleep. If you go to sleep now, Jorge, I will take you to the movies at nine o'clock."

"O.K.," said Jorge. Then he said to Candita, "My room is 212. I will wait for you tomorrow, Candita. When the bell rings, I will be at the door of my room." Jorge ran out.

Margarita said, "Mrs. Torres, how will Jorge get up tomorrow morning to go to school if he goes to the movies at nine o'clock this evening?"

Mrs. Torres looked unhappy. "It is not right, I know. But, Margarita, see—all day there is the factory and my mother even when she is at home falls asleep at once after supper and as we have no television, I go to the movies, where I can forget the machines of the factory and all the troubles with Paco and the jobs he does not keep and, anyway, Jorge can sleep in the movie as at home and—"

Mama came in with a shopping bag full of groceries. Jorge came running back.

"Now that you are both here," Mama said, "and as we are going to have our supper at once and you are our neighbors, we invite you and your little boy to join us. There is enough for all."

"O.K. We stay here," Jorge said.

"Thank you," said Mrs. Torres. "Tonight we will not go to the movies. We will go Friday when Jorge can sleep late the next day. Margarita, you are like the lady of the school when you speak of the movies. Do you know the lady of the school, Mrs. Rivera?"

"I have heard of her," said Mama, "but I do not know her."

"She speaks of Jorge and the movies as Margarita does and she speaks in Spanish. Also she has asked to see Jorge's father, but how can I tell Paco to go to see her if I myself do not speak to him and he does not live here and it is much better, I can tell you, that he does not and—"

"Maybe he will come back soon," said Jorge.

Mrs. Torres and Jorge ate their supper with the Rivera family. Jorge, while eating, talked about his teacher. "This is a very strict teacher. No guy can punch another guy in the class," said Jorge. Jorge sometimes spoke English and sometimes Spanish. Candita understood Jorge in either language.

Mama said after they left, "Candita, it was kind to say you would help Mrs. Torres with Jorge." Mama went on, "Jorge is a boy one must watch closely. He can easily hurt himself climbing or running about. If you find it difficult to take care of him after school, we will have to tell Mrs. Torres. It is a great responsibility to take care of a boy who is even a little wild." Mama added, "But Jorge's mother has many troubles. You do well to help her, Candita."

70

9

CANDITA looked into Room 212. Jorge was not there. She walked downstairs and then outside. She looked at the faces of a crowd of children standing in a circle to watch two boys wrestling. The two who were wrestling

rolled toward her and she saw that one of them was Jorge Torres.

"Jorge!"

Jorge looked up with his arm around the neck of the other boy. Jorge let go and scrambled up. "O.K. Come on, Candita." He smiled at her. "Come on home, Candita."

"Why are you fighting?"

"I am not fighting," said Jorge. "This is my friend. He is Alberto."

Alberto disappeared.

"Jorge, you must go back and wash your hands and your face, too."

"O.K." Jorge ran inside the school. His face was much cleaner when he came out. He had wet the top of his head, too, and had combed his hair with his fingers.

Jorge looked into store windows on the way. He showed Candita the things he wanted: hardware supplies, electric fixtures, fruit from the grocery, cakes.

"When I have much money," said Jorge, speaking English only, "when I am a big man, I will buy fifty chocolate cakes. Large ones."

Jorge spread his arms to cover the whole store front. "I will eat fifty chocolate cakes."

"If you eat too much, you will be sick."

"No," said Jorge, standing still and staring at the cakes. "Not me. I am never sick. I am a tough guy. My father says I am a tough guy. You see this cake? My father will buy me this cake if I ask him. My father is a very millionaire guy."

"I have a book," said Candita, showing it to Jorge. "If you will come home now, I will read the story for you. This is a very good story."

"O.K.," said Jorge agreeably, not moving away from in front of the cakes, "read the story."

"I will read it when we are at home and you are sitting down and listening to this story."

Jorge left the bakery window. He hopped on one foot for a half block, then ran from store window to store window, or lagged behind, or ran ahead of Candita. Mama said yesterday it was a great responsibility to take care of a boy like Jorge. Candita saw she would have to tell Mrs. Torres to look for someone else to take care of him.

74

When they reached home and walked up-stairs, she held Jorge by the hand. Otherwise he would surely run down again and disappear. While she was unlocking the door, he slipped his hand out of hers, but instead of running downstairs he ran to his own door and banged on it. Then he ran back to Candita.

"What is this story?" Jorge said coming into the apartment with her.

She read Jorge the whole story of Bushy Tail. She hardly had to glance at the words. Jorge asked her to read it to him once more. After she read it again, Jorge asked for it over again.

"No," Candita said, "that is enough for this story of Bushy Tail."

"Then read another one," said Jorge. "Read another story."

Candita said in Spanish, "One day a squirrel was going to the factory to work. On the way he met a boy whose name was Alberto. 'I want to see a large animal, Alberto,' said the squirrel. 'So far I have seen only squirrels in the park and cats and dogs in the streets of New York. Do you know where I can find a large animal?'

" 'Yes,' Alberto said, 'go to the zoo.'

" 'Which animals does one find in the zoo?' said the squirrel.

" 'Large ones,' said Alberto. 'Like the giraffe. Once you observe a giraffe you will know an animal with the longest neck in the world.' "

"Show me a giraffe," said Jorge.

Candita looked for a sheet of paper and then drew a giraffe such as she had seen in the zoo and such as Alvaro had made in school.

"This animal makes me laugh," said Jorge. "Tell me what happened."

"The little squirrel went to the zoo and there he found the giraffe. He looked at the giraffe and he said to himself, 'This giraffe has a fine long neck, but his tail is nothing. I prefer my tail to his neck.' "

Jorge said, "Draw me another giraffe."

Candita drew another giraffe with an even longer neck. Jorge laughed at this one also.

Candita said, "Would you like to put spots on him? Like this." She showed Jorge how to

76

put spots on the giraffe and Jorge put spots on him. When he was through putting spots on the giraffe, he continued to put them all over the paper.

"The spots are only on the giraffe," Candita said, "and not around him."

She was surprised to see it was almost five o'clock.

"Tell me another story," said Jorge.

"Once there was an airplane," she said, "an ordinary airplane that flew from the airport of New York. A girl whose name was Candita and a boy named Jorge flew in this plane. It arrived at Mayagüez, the neighborhood of Buena Vista. 'Here we shall stay,' the girl said. 'It is the best place in the world.'"

"I have heard of Mayagüez," said Jorge.

A key was turned in the lock. Mama came in. In her hand she carried a shopping bag full of green vegetables.

A moment later Mrs. Torres arrived.

"This is for taking care of Jorge," Mrs. Torres said, searching in her handbag and bringing out a yard of red ribbon. "And for you, Jorge, for being good, here is a bag of candy."

Jorge emptied the bag on the table. Gumdrops of every color rolled out.

Candita held the ribbon against her hair. She looked into the mirror. "Mrs. Torres, I thank you for this ribbon."

"It is nothing," said Mrs. Torres. "You have befriended me, Candita. You have kept me from too much worry over Jorge. Jorge, come home. It is now time to leave."

"One moment," said Jorge. "I will come after I eat this candy."

"No," said Mrs. Torres, "this candy is not to be eaten all at once."

"Mrs. Torres," Candita said, remembering that she herself had worried over Jorge, "I do not think that tomorrow—"

"Jorge," said Mrs. Torres, "if you go home now, Candita will come in the morning, too, and take you to school—and bring you back— take you and bring you."

Candita looked at Mrs. Torres' happy face.

She said to Jorge, "Yes, I will come and get you in the morning. I will see you in the morning, Jorge, if you go home now."

"O.K.," said Jorge, as he left.

10

THE NEXT MORNING when Candita
knocked, Mrs. Torres came to the door. She
shook her head when she saw Candita. "Ah,
Candita, he is sick. I have made a terrible mis-
take. It was this candy. He ate it all. And not
only is he sick but it is his birthday. Jorge is

sick on his birthday. You must go to school by yourself. I will stay home. Today I do not go to the factory. I will take care of Jorge."

Candita hurried to school. This morning she carried along the little carving of Renaldo's to show to Miss Singer.

Miss Singer put Renaldo's rabbit between Candita's clay squirrel and clay dog and invited the children to look closely at it. Everyone slid fingers over the smooth carving and turned it about.

All through the day Candita's eyes traveled to the window sill. Renaldo, who was so far away, now had his rabbit in her classroom. She told Linda, during lunch, about Renaldo's house and of the picture he had made of her with a flower in her hair.

At the end of the day Miss Singer said, "Thank you for bringing the little rabbit, Candita. It makes our room the most beautiful in the school. I wish we could have it for a few days. May we?" Even in Spanish Miss Singer talked more patiently to Candita than to anyone else.

"I will be glad to leave it here," Candita said in Spanish also.

"We are truly grateful, Candita."

Candita walked home quickly today because of Jorge. She meant to knock at the Torreses' door to find out if he were better, but by the time she had come to the second floor, she knew it was the Torres family they were all talking about.

By the time she had arrived at her own floor, Candita had heard the whole story.

As the weather was hot, all the doors in the hallway remained open. She could recognize each voice.

Old Mrs. Ranchera called out to someone, "Now it will be a long time before the family is at peace again. It is unfortunate!"

"Do you say unfortunate? It is a disaster! But you know, Grandmother, he should not have come at all."

"It was only to bring a little present," said Mrs. Gomez from across the hall.

"Did you see the present?" asked still another voice.

"No, not I. Clara is the one who saw it."

"Yes, I saw it."

"Describe it, then, for me."

"It was a little Madonna, white and blue. Small and perfect."

Mrs. Ranchera sighed so loudly Candita could hear it all the way up on the next floor.

"But to have a pistol is a very bad thing," said Mrs. Calles.

"The mother's duty," another raised voice answered sternly, "is to let the child receive a present from the father, no matter whether the father is separated from the family or not. Have in mind, he is still the father."

On the next floor Candita heard the story all over again. A relative had come to visit Mrs. Gonzalez and she was telling the story to her visitor: "This family lives on the fifth floor," said Mrs. Gonzalez.

Candita climbed the fourth flight of stairs.

" . . . she works in a factory. He has one job one day and the next day another job. She tells him, and I have heard them quarreling, 'You must work at one thing. Jorge will learn

bad habits from you if he sees you go from one factory to another.' Then, suddenly, this man leaves his family.

"Today he returns. He returns bringing a Madonna to his little son for a birthday present. He cannot allow the day to pass without seeing his son. What does the mother do? She says to the little boy, who is recovering from a sickness, 'You must refuse this present.'

"The little boy obeys. What does the father do? He takes a pistol and shoots. There is a terrible noise. She cannot stop screaming. A policeman runs to the scene."

"Ah," said the visitor, a lady with a deep voice. "It is always better for the mother to say nothing. The best would be to accept the present. Everything can be arranged later."

"True, Juanita," Mrs. Gonzalez said. "This woman is wrong. But you have asked me to tell you the story and this is the story."

"Also, there is this. To have a pistol one must have a license," said Juanita, her visitor.

"The pistol is the bad thing," said Mrs. Gonzalez. "The pistol without the license. At this moment the Torres family, mother, father, and son, are in the police station."

Candita ran up the last flight of stairs.

The Torreses' door was locked. No one answered her knock.

The voices in the hall were still talking about the Torres family when Mama came home.

"Did you hear, Mama? They are talking about Jorge and his mother and—"

"I have heard," said Mama. "I have never seen the police station, but I know it is not good for this boy to be there. Today I have read about the lady of the social service. Wait, Candita, I want to look at this newspaper again."

Mama found the newspaper she had brought home. "Yes, here it is. The story is of a Mrs. Santos, who went for a walk. When she returned, she did not recognize her own house, for all the houses seemed alike to her in this city. As she was lost, she was taken to the police station. Then the lady of the social service spoke over the radio. The daughter of the lost Mrs. Santos heard the radio speech and came to the police station. There she recovered her mother."

"But Jorge is not lost."

"It is true, but perhaps the lady of the social service will help us, too. Perhaps she will ask them to let Jorge come home to us. At least he will not sleep in the police station." Mama looked at the newspaper once more. "Here is the address. Someone will tell us how to find it."

Mama was writing the address. The room was quiet. Outside, a woman's voice called, "Estrellita! Estrellita!" and a girl's voice answered, "One moment, one moment, I am coming!" A baby was crying on the floor below, and Mr. Calles was practicing on his guitar. Through the open window all the sounds of late afternoon, familiar now to Candita, were heard by her separately and together.

"It is well I am home early," said Mama. "I would like to bring Jorge here."

Candita looked about her. In the center of the table a green vase held some of the paper flowers that Fernanda and Mama made at the factory. The flowers looked better than real flowers. The roses were larger than real roses, and the daisies were larger than the daisies of the fields and in the flower stores. The white carnations were giants of white carnations. Yes, better to bring Jorge here than to leave him in the police station, whatever that was.

Together they went down the stairs. Smells of the evening cooking were beginning to fill the narrow hallway, garlic and chili and freshly sliced pineapple.

On the way down Mama asked Mrs. Gonzalez how to find the address on the card.

"It is around the corner," said Mrs. Gonzalez. "First go to the right, then go to the left, and you are there!"

Mama and Candita walked along the street, which was crowded with children. Their mothers every now and then called to them not to get hurt or lost, to stop fighting, to keep from falling.

11

MRS. D'ALVAREZ had not yet gone home. She was alone in a small square room with a desk in the center that was almost as large as the room. On this immense desk, a single pink carnation stood on its thin green stem in a glass of water. A true carnation. Its sweet clove scent filled the air.

Mrs. d'Alvarez listened to Mama and looked

more and more disturbed over the story of the Torres family.

"Ah, yes, the parents are themselves like children. We must be patient with these parents as with children," Mrs. d'Alvarez said impatiently. She lifted the telephone. "I will try to explain this to the police station."

Mama said, "Is it possible to take this little boy, Jorge Torres, home with us, as we are the neighbors of this family? He can wait for his mother at our house."

Mrs. d'Alvarez raised her shoulders, nodded, then raised her shoulders again, all while beginning to speak hastily into the telephone.

Candita looked around. On one wall of Mrs. d'Alvarez' office hung a map of *The Island of Puerto Rico*. The island looked small. Surrounding it and covering most of the map was a blue expanse with the words *Atlantic Ocean* printed across it. The tiny word *Mayagüez* appeared on the island with a dot beside it. She had come from that dot across that enormous blue distance!

Mrs. d'Alvarez talked rapidly in English. She nodded each time she said, "Yes, yes," into the telephone. When she finished her conversation, she turned to Mama. She clasped her hands together.

"Do not worry about Jorge Torres. Nor about his parents. It is as I said. Those two are people who are like children. Even this pistol that has made so much trouble is discovered to be a toy. I would not be surprised if Jorge is already at home when you return. And his mother, too."

"We will go and see," Mama said, well pleased. "Thank you, thank you."

As they hurried home they passed the A. & P. Candita saw Rafael and Barnabe, who were boxing.

"Hello, Candita," Rafael called. "I am making money. I deliver the groceries in my delivery wagon." Rafael stopped boxing and pointed to a sagging baby carriage.

"Hello, Rafael."

"This afternoon I have already made thirty-five cents."

"And I, also, thirty-five cents," said Barnabe. "We are using the same delivery wagon."

91

"Good," she said. "That is very good."

The boys had spoken in English and she had answered in English. It was the first time anyone in her class had heard her speak English, but neither Barnabe nor Rafael had noticed.

Candita and Mama turned the corner. Just as Mrs. d'Alvarez had said, there was Mrs. Torres and Jorge and Jorge's grandmother, too, home from the hospital, and talking to a few neighbors.

Mrs. Torres ran to Mama. "I am sorry. I cannot help screaming when there is a loud noise—to scream has always been my habit since I was small—that is why they have arrested him and now they are keeping him in the police station, but an official has telephoned and after this everything has improved and—"

Mama said, "We have just come from Mrs. d'Alvarez, the lady of the social service. She has promised to help."

"Mrs. d'Alvarez?" asked Mrs. Torres excitedly. "I have heard that when Mrs. d'Alvarez says she will help someone it is as if it were already done."

92

The grandmother looked at Mrs. Torres as if she had won a prize.

"We thank you, Mrs. Rivera," the grandmother said. "We thank you for your kindness. We did not know who had telephoned, but after the telephone call all became better. We thank you for your friendship to us. Were it not for you, we, together with Paco, would still have been sitting in the police station."

"Let us all go upstairs," said Mama. "There has been too much confusion today."

"Do you want to come with me, Jorge?" Candita asked him.

Jorge put his hand into Candita's. At the second set of stairs, Jorge said, "I want to hear again about the giraffe. Read to me about the giraffe, Candita."

Mrs. Torres and the grandmother and Mama followed Candita and Jorge into the Riveras' apartment. Jorge's mother and grandmother were as interested as Jorge in the giraffe, who in Candita's story was taking a ride in the subway.

Mama was putting a pot on the stove. "There is enough for all," Mama said. "There is enough for us and for you, Mrs. Torres, and for your mother and for Jorge. Later on, when it is time for Jorge to go to sleep, you will all go home."

Mrs. Torres nodded absently, still listening to Candita's story.

Everyone could not be seated at the table at once. Candita and Jorge and the two little girls and Fernanda had their supper first. While the children were eating, there was a knock at the door.

Mama went to open it.

"I am Mr. Torres. It is not my fault—"

Jorge ran to him.

Mr. Torres put his arm around Jorge's shoulders. "It is not his fault and it is not my fault. It is perhaps not anyone's fault, but it is because of this birthday present for Jorge—"

"Sit down," said Mama. "There is enough for all. You must be tired and hungry. We understand how all of this happened. Everything will be arranged."

Late in the evening, Jorge and his mother, his father and his grandmother went home together.

12

MISS SINGER said, "Who will go to the blackboard?"

Rafael raised his hand.

"Good. Rafael may write on the board."

Miss Singer said the words for Rafael and Rafael wrote them on the blackboard. He wrote *Tuesday* and *squirrel* and *house* and *train* and *plane.*

They were words that Candita knew and could write, too, but it would be different, she thought, if the whole class were watching her. At the blackboard she would surely forget how to write them.

"Very good. Erase the words, please. *Erase.*" Miss Singer made the motion of erasing. "This is your last week here, Rafael," said Miss Singer. "Next week you are going up to Miss Wood's class. Will anyone else go to the blackboard?"

Candita looked down at her desk.

"Alvaro," said Miss Singer.

Alvaro went to the blackboard and wrote three words. All were right.

One day, Candita thought, she would surprise Miss Singer. It would not be tomorrow. It would not be next week. It would be one day a long time from now.

That day Miss Singer would ask a question in English, as always. On that day she, Candita, would raise her hand. Miss Singer would call on her and she would stand up and speak in English. Everyone would turn around. . . .'

The bell rang for lunch.

Today she did not feel hungry. She sat listening to the others begin to talk loudly in Spanish, and heard the rattling of the papers as sandwiches were unwrapped. The room was too warm, although no one else seemed to notice this.

Another thing—once she began to speak English, she would never again speak Spanish at lunch time. She would do exactly what Miss Singer did. She would let the others speak Spanish, but she, Candita, would answer in English.

"Candita," Miss Singer said, still speaking Spanish, "please take this paper to the office of the principal."

Candita was glad to go out into the cool hall. She ran all the way downstairs and took the paper into Mrs. Peterson's office.

On the way back she walked more slowly. Running had given her a sharp pain in her side.

Candita came back into the classroom. Some

of the boys had already finished lunch and now were carrying the record player to the center of the room. Luis was putting on his favorite records, reading their titles aloud to the class. *"España Cañí!"* he shouted. "The Stars and the Stripes Forever!"

Today Luis was choosing the noisiest ones.

The room was even warmer than it had been, and the music sounded louder and louder. Candita was as tired as if she had run a race.

She put her head on her folded arms on her desk, and shut her eyes. The whole room boomed and echoed with the noisy music. At the same time the pain in her side was beginning once more. It was suddenly sharper and more important than any other thing. It was as if it had always been there. She could not remember a time when there had not been this pain in her side.

Miss Singer was at her desk, but it was better not to tell her about this. Miss Singer would surely say, "Tell me in English, Candita." She tried to think about the words she must use to say that something hurt. Miss Singer would laugh at her. That would be the worst of all. If Miss Singer laughed at her, the children would surely laugh, too.

Perhaps it would be well to find Linda. Was Linda absent today? She did not remember seeing her. She tried to lift her head, but it was not possible. Instead she let her head rest on

99

her folded arms and kept her eyes closed.

She waited for the bell to ring. When the bell rang, she would get up and hurry home. Mama would put her to bed and give her a medicine and in the morning she would come back to school and no one would know that it had hurt so much she could not sit up.

Someone put a hand lightly on her shoulder. "Candita, are you asleep?"

She shook her head slowly.

It was Miss Singer, and it was a good thing that she was not speaking English but Spanish. "Does something hurt?"

"Yes," she answered in Spanish, too. "Something hurts here." She put her hand to her side and she said, "Will the bell ring soon? I would like to go home."

"Can you stand up?" Miss Singer asked.

"Soon," said Candita. "I will stand up soon."

"You don't have to wait for the bell to ring if you want to go home."

She had not thought she could go home before the bell rang. She said, "Then I will go

100

now." She tried to stand and Miss Singer held her hand securely as Mama did, but when she stood up, it was too much. The pain was too great and she sat again.

"Sit quietly, then," said Miss Singer.

"I will surely go when the bell rings," said Candita. "I will get up then."

"Put your head down again, Candita. You won't have to walk all the way home."

"It is not far."

Miss Singer put her hand lightly on Candita's forehead, and then stroked her hair.

Then she heard Miss Singer's footsteps going away. She heard her say to the others, "You must let Candita rest. She does not feel well, so do not try to talk to her or make her stand up. I will be out of the room for a moment. Please play the records softly. Linda, take my place, please, until I return."

Then—but it was a long time later—Miss Singer came back.

The children's voices seemed far away. The music had stopped.

"Someone went to your house, Candita, to

look for your mother. No one is at home. We will take you to the hospital, Candita. We have left a note for your mother. Candita, try not to cry."

She was crying for many reasons. Because Miss Singer was speaking softly and in Spanish. And because the children did not come to her. And because she was thinking that perhaps she was going to die and they would never know—no one would ever know, especially Miss Singer would never know—that she could say almost all the words of *Bushy Tail the Squirrel*. It was only that she had been waiting until she could say the words even better. And, also, she was crying because the pain seemed to be in her whole body, not only in her side but everywhere, in her head and behind her eyes, too.

The pain was leaving. She sat up. She said to Miss Singer, who continued to sit beside her, "I will go home now. Here, around my neck, is the key to my house."

Miss Singer shook her head as if she knew that just then the pain was beginning again.

102

A man came into the room and lifted her up as if she were a little baby and as gently as if he knew how great the pain was. He carried her downstairs and into an automobile, and inside the automobile was Mrs. Peterson.

Once, a long time ago, when they had gone to San Juan, someone had taken her and Mama for a ride in an automobile. She wished she could keep her eyes open now and see the New York streets as she had seen the streets of San Juan, but the pain did not allow it.

She kept her eyes closed, and after the automobile stopped, again she was carried in secure strong arms.

"Candita, you are at the hospital now." It was Mrs. Peterson who held her hand. "They will see what is wrong and make you well. As soon as possible your mother will come to see you. I will stay with you until then." Mrs. Peterson, too, spoke quietly in Spanish.

Candita opened her eyes.

This was the hospital. This was where Mrs. Torres' mother had been when she had been sick. This was what the inside of the hospital looked like and smelled like. A strong smell, cool and sharp as of many medicines . . .

Mrs. Peterson was still holding her hand. But it was not Mrs. Peterson. It was someone else. A girl with serious dark eyes. The girl gently released Candita's hand. Quickly she untied Candita's sneakers and slipped them off, and unbuttoned Candita's dress.

Now there was no longer pain. There was only deep sleep.

13

SHE KNEW she was dreaming, for she was back in Mayagüez and sitting on the doorstep of their little house. She was reading aloud. There was Jorge beside her and there was Mrs. Torres and her mother, and also there was the lady of the social service. They were listening to her as she read the whole book of *Bushy Tail the Squirrel* to them. She had never read it so well.

It was curious. She read the whole book and did not once have to look at the words to remember them.

Jorge said, "Again, Candita."

She put the book down and told Jorge the story again, word for word.

Then, a long time later, she heard Mama's voice. "The doctor says Candita will soon awaken and we may stay so that we will be the first to talk to her."

It was Fernanda's voice that answered. "I have inquired from the nurse. She called this sickness ap-pendi-ci-tis."

"I have heard of ap-pendi-ci-tis," said Mama. "It is a very big thing."

"It was necessary to make this operation at once. They were afraid it was already late. We are fortunate it was not late."

Mama said, "The doctor said she will be well. I said to this doctor, 'You can be truthful with me. I am strong enough to hear even bad news, for I have lighted a candle and I have prayed.'"

Mama was frightened, although she was

106

saying she was strong. Candita wanted to tell her at once not to be frightened.

She opened her eyes. The ceiling of this room seemed far away and shadowy.

"How are you, Candita?" Mama was standing beside her. "Tell me how you feel."

Candita took a deep breath and found she could speak. "It does not hurt now," she said.

"Thank God. Now you will be well. I have lighted a candle and I have prayed and I have the promise of the doctor. Soon Renaldo will be here, Candita."

"Renaldo?"

Mama was holding her hand. "Candita, I must tell you one thing. I must tell you, first, that I love you. Candita, I love you as if you were my own child. Yet you are not. Your own mother died, Candita, when you were two weeks old. Renaldo was so young then, so alone and so helpless himself, he could not care for you."

"Renaldo? Renaldo is my father?"

"Yes, Candita, my child. Your mother said to me, 'You and José are my neighbors and my

107

friends. I do not think I shall die, Rosita. I want to live and take care of my baby and my husband, but I must tell you this, that if some accident should happen and I should not live, please take this baby. I would like to name her Candelaria after our blessed saint.' Do you hear, Candita?"

"Yes, Mama."

"I would not have told you, Candita, for many years. Perhaps I would never have told you this, for you know in our country it is not unusual to be of a family without being born into it. We love little children so much we cannot bear to let them be brought up without a mother. Yet, when you were so sick, I thought Renaldo should come. We sent a telegram to Renaldo. He is already on his way here."

Fernanda bent over her. "Candita, we all love you. We all have missed you. How small you look in this large bed. Do you know who has missed you most? I think Jorge has missed you the most. When you come home, we will have a celebration, even bigger than when you arrived. The whole house will come this time."

Mama said, "One must recover entirely before one can have a true celebration."

The door opened and the nurse, looking in, said, "This little girl is tired. You can come again tomorrow. *Mañana, mañana!*"

Mama nodded and sighed deeply and said to Fernanda, "I can sleep this night, for I have seen Candita and I have heard her speak to us."

14

WHEN Mama and Fernanda had gone, a girl in a faded blue uniform came in.

"I've come to see you awake. Up to now I've only seen you asleep. How are you feeling?"

"I think I am better. Thank you," Candita said, in English, too, before she knew she was speaking English.

"Soon you'll be moved out of this room into a room with other children. That's the ward. But while you are alone the nurse sent me here —that's if you want me—for company."

"I want you—yes."

"My name is Jeanie."

Candita remembered something. "You are the one who took me to the room with the strong light, no?"

"The operating room," Jeanie said. "I took you from there, too. You told me a long story."

"I told you a story?"

"About Bushy Tail the Squirrel. It was as long as a book."

"It is a book."

"Do you learn every word in all the books you read?"

"It is the first I have read in English."

"The first! You told it as if you'd known English all your life."

Candita held her breath and felt her heart begin to pound. It was as she had hoped. Only she had hoped it would be Miss Singer who would say it.

"I have just learned," Candita said.

She had known it would be this way. She could say anything she wanted to say. Almost anything. It would still be difficult to talk about some things, but she could try. There was something she wanted to ask of Jeanie—she would remember what it was when she was not so tired.

The light from beside ·the bed fell on Jeanie's cheek and chin. Jeanie looked like someone else, someone she had already seen in some other place.

"You don't have to talk, Candita. I'll talk to you. I'll tell you how I happen to be here, shall I?"

"Yes, yes."

Jeanie said softly, "I read a book once about a man who saved the lives of many sick people. I was about your age then. His name was Louis Pasteur. I decided to do work like his."

"The work of a doctor?"

"I would like to be a doctor. A children's doctor."

Jeanie's hands were small, but strong, too. Candita nodded.

"This is the beginning of my school vacation," Jeanie said. "I'm trying to learn all I can here at the hospital. Candita—I nearly forgot what I was sent in to ask you—is there something you would like? Something to drink?"

"No, thank you."

What she wanted was nothing to drink or eat. It was the little wood rabbit she had brought to school. She would have liked it here on the dresser where she could look at it, or beside her on this small table. Thinking of the carving made her think of Renaldo and now, at last, she knew what it was she wanted to ask Jeanie, if the right words could be found.

I will ask tomorrow, she thought. I will find the right words tomorrow. It might have been a dream. But if it were true, could Jeanie tell her? Her head felt heavy.

A nurse came in and put a thin pencil of glass into her mouth. In a little while she removed the thin glass and wrote on a long paper and then spoke in a low voice to Jeanie.

"I must go now, Miss Bevis says. Good night, Candita."

15

IT WAS MORNING. This room, too, was warm, as warm as the classroom had been the last day she had been at school.

Miss Singer stood at the door. She unfolded a paper as large as a newspaper and held it up for Candita to see. On it were drawings of flowers and birds, a giraffe and a squirrel, and in and out among the animals and around them in the margins, the children of her class had written their names. *Rafael*, she read, *Linda, Barnabe*, and all the others. On top, in red, were the words HASTA LA VISTA, CANDITA.

"Your five minutes are up," the nurse said.

"She will like this, I think," Miss Singer whispered, "when she is better."

The nurse took the paper and thumbtacks from Miss Singer and tacked the paper on the wall, while Miss Singer looked back from the door.

Miss Singer was leaving, and Candita had to ask a great favor of her.

"Miss Singer!" she called loudly. It surprised her to hear how small a sound she made.

"May I?" Miss Singer asked the nurse, as if Miss Singer were a little girl in a class and the nurse were the teacher.

"Just for a second only."

Miss Singer tiptoed to the bed.

Candita said in Spanish, "Is the little rabbit still in the classroom? I would like to look at it, please."

115

"I'll bring it to you, Candita. I promise."

Outside the window the light faded into evening, and then into night. Then gray as of early morning, and later, darkness again. Once, and again, and again.

Of them all—Mama, Fernanda, Jeanie, Miss Singer—only Miss Bevis, the nurse, came to see her.

"You must rest. You were tired yesterday. And the day before," Miss Bevis said. "Perhaps tomorrow you may have visitors."

But the next day it was the same.

Great splashing drops washed against the window in changing watery patterns. There on the wall was the sheet of paper Miss Singer had brought with the children's writing and drawings on it. It was the only friendly thing.

I must be very sick, she thought, if no one is allowed to come to see me.

She heard the door open and turned her head. Jeanie was coming in. In her hand was Renaldo's rabbit.

"I'm not supposed to be here, but this was downstairs looking lonely. Miss Singer left it for you."

Jeanie set it on the little table beside the bed. It was another friendly thing. And Jeanie was here. Yes, she was very sick, she thought, to judge by the heaviness in her head. She was very sick because she was too tired to ask the question of Jeanie.

She wanted to lie quietly and to look at the little rabbit and to go to sleep. And she was too tired, too, to tell Jeanie that her face had been known to her for a long time, for it was like the round-faced statue in the soft light of the candles in the little church of Mayagüez.

Jeanie bent over her. "Candita, please get well. In the book outside it says that your father is coming. He can come in at any time to see you—the minute he comes."

It was not a dream. It was true. Renaldo was coming.

Miss Bevis came in. When she had looked at the thin glass of the thermometer, she said,

"That is much better. Much, much better."

But Candita already knew she was much better. She was no longer tired.

"Let me sit up," Candita said, "please let me."

"Not yet," said the nurse. "Not quite yet. We have been very sick. But tomorrow we shall be quite a bit better."

16

JEANIE came early the next morning. To please her, Candita ate all the food on her tray, the new things—dry grain in a bowl and golden sauce in a glass dish.

Jeanie sat on the arm of the chair beside Candita's bed. Between them, on the table, stood Renaldo's rabbit. Jeanie ran a finger over it.

"It is the work of my father," said Candita. It was easy to say, and it was the first time. "His name is Renaldo—Renaldo Montez."

"Your father carved the rabbit? He is talented! Candita, have you ever been to a museum?"

"No."

"My father works in one. It's a place where you can see how all living things began, animals and people. My father designs the exhibits. In a way, he's an artist, too, though I don't think he can carve. When I was small, I used to ask my father for some of his paints. I tried to paint, but I had to give up. Later I began to read about people who could do other things."

"Did you ever try to make figures of clay?" Candita asked her. "I made some that are on the window sill of my class."

"Do your little figures do what you want them to do? When I paint or draw, they never come out right," Jeanie said.

"Not always, but sometimes. Yes, sometimes."

Jeanie reached into her pocket and took out

120

a notebook. "You had a high fever, Candita, but now you're getting well so fast they aren't even bothering to put you into the ward. I'm afraid I'll come back after having a day off and find you gone. I better write your address here. You must promise to write me after I write you."

"Yes, I will write you. And you will tell me when you are a doctor."

"It will be a long time from now. Three more years of college, then four years of medical school, and then—" Jeanie laughed. "Candita, you will be as old as I am now when I am a doctor."

"You do not look old, Jeanie. You do not look as old as Fernanda. Fernanda is eighteen."

"I'll be eighteen soon," Jeanie said. "Is Fernanda your big sister?"

"Yes. Fernanda is different from you. She is pretty, too, but different. She is always laughing."

"And you are the way I used to be at eleven, Candita. Solemn. Candita, teach me some

Spanish words so I can talk to sick little Spanish children."

"I will teach you enough for conversations with very little children. *Yes* is *sí*, and *no* is *no*. *Please* is *por favor* and *thank you very much* is *muchas gracias* and *no sé* means *I don't know.*"

Jeanie learned quickly—she learned five more phrases after the first five, and five after those.

All the time that Jeanie was learning Spanish words, Candita was thinking, When will Renaldo come? Perhaps in a moment. Now. He will open the door now. I have not seen him for a long time. I have not walked with him on Sunday for a long time.

Miss Bevis, after lunch, was teaching Candita to walk. She had completely forgotten how.

She stood up and the room began slowly to sail around her. She leaned on Miss Bevis. Miss Bevis said, "Steady. Try it alone. Now, Candita."

She could walk no better than Martina at first. And then—then it was as it had always

122

been. She could walk again. It was only when she had learned to walk again by herself that Miss Bevis let her go back to bed. She was as tired as if she had walked all day. She slept soundly, and when she opened her eyes, Mama and Renaldo were there.

He had changed. Or perhaps here he looked different than in Mayagüez, where she had last seen him. Against the white hospital wall his face looked known and unknown to her at the same time. She studied his straight thin features. They were a little like his own carvings, delicate and definite, at the same time. She could see something else. She could see that his eyes were like hers. She could see the resemblance between them. It surprised her and made her happy.

"Are you well again, Candita?"

"I am better now. You have come a long distance."

"It is nothing," Renaldo said. "The distance is nothing."

"I have now brought Renaldo to you," said Mama, "and I must go back to the factory. He will tell you—" Mama sighed a long deep sigh "—better than I can what he has wanted to tell you so long. He will tell you of Yolanda, your mother, who was frail as a flower and beautiful as a flower."

Mama brought to Candita's bedside a pink carnation she had herself made.

"Fernanda will come later to take Renaldo home to us," she said.

When Mama left, Renaldo said, "It is true what you have heard of Yolanda. You are much like her, Candita, but not so frail. There is much to tell you of the songs she loved to sing, and of our plans for you."

Renaldo put a paper-wrapped package on the bedside table. "Candita, I hope you will like this as much as the other." He was looking at his rabbit on the table.

She carefully unfolded the wrappings.

It was the carving of a little cat, proud as any lion.

"It is as beautiful as the first," she said. "Renaldo, I would like to try to carve."

"I have the little figure you gave me. I will

help you, Candita. It will be easy for you. I have seen how you work with clay."

"You truly think it will be easy for me?"

"I think so, yes. Before I leave for Mayagüez, I will tell you the little I myself know of carving."

She tried not to show her disappointment. "You have not come to stay?"

Renaldo shook his head slowly. "It would be difficult to stay. Yet, when I see you, I want to stay."

She said, "Then I will go back with you, Renaldo."

He looked at her in silence, and in concern.

"I can take good care of your house, Renaldo. I can learn to cook. I have a friend who has learned. And I want to learn how to carve."

"It is best that you stay here, Candita. You need better care than I can give you. Candita, the opportunities are here. You are beginning with an education. I did not." Renaldo put his hand on his carved cat, and Candita saw that his hands were as work-roughened as Pedro Chavez' hands.

"I must go back alone, Candita. Here I could only do the work of a laborer. I could use only the strength of my body, nothing else, for I have had no education, nor do I know the language. I would work all day long and there would no longer be time for this." Again his hand rested on his carving.

"I will come with you. I would like to be in Mayagüez again."

Someone knocked lightly and came into the room. It was Fernanda.

"Renaldo!" Fernanda said. "I have not seen you in many years. You are not at all changed. Candita, how are you? You are almost well—it is as if you had never been sick. You are perhaps a little thin, but Mama will soon give you proper food."

Miss Bevis opened the door. "Candita has learned to walk all over again today. She is tired. Day after tomorrow she goes home. You'll have her all to yourselves then. Say good night to her now."

In a few minutes, as soon as Mama and

Renaldo and Fernanda would come, she would leave the hospital.

She sat waiting for them in the chair beside the bed she had occupied so many days. She had, in those days, learned each corner of the room—the pattern of the flowers on the chair she was sitting in, the pattern of the white bedspread. She had thought it was an immense high-ceilinged room. It was small. Even the ceiling was not high.

Jeanie came hurrying in. "I thought I was too late to say good-by. Miss Bevis said, 'Our Candita is getting ready to leave.' "

"Jeanie, I am glad you came. Thank you for so much kindness." Candita's eyes fell on the cat. "I now have two. It is possible I shall not see you again, Jeanie. Take it then. You will think of me when you see it, no?"

"Can you really part with it? It's something you love. And what will your father say when you tell him you've given away his cat?"

"I would like you to keep it. I think he will understand."

"Thank you, Candita." Jeanie held the cat

cradled in her hands. "You look solemn today. What are you thinking about?"

"My father is going back to Puerto Rico. I want to go with him—to live in his house and learn his work, and then to cook and to sew for him."

"Now that he is here, Candita, perhaps he'll change his mind. He may want to stay."

"There is no work for him here. At home,

before the sun rises he goes out to work in the fields. Later, when the sun is high, he does this work, the work of carving that he loves. He cannot change."

"You won't stay in New York without him, Candita?"

"I want to stay if he will stay. If he does not—"

"You want to go with him."

"Yes, yes."

"Candita, it isn't easy to take care of a house, even a small one. I've tried, too. Some of the little time he has will be spent worrying over you, because he'd be trying to take good care of you. Candita, are you sure there will be enough money for both of you?"

No. She was not sure of any of these things. Jeanie, who made everything better always, was not making anything better now.

"Write me, Candita. Here is my address. Write me if you go away."

"Yes, Jeanie. Thank you again. For everything."

17

ONCE MORE, at the Riveras', the apartment had been made ready to welcome Candita. The pink and blue crepe-paper streamers were there decorating the ceiling as before. Today there were no loud joyous greetings, no dancing around the room.

Everyone was quiet. Even Martina and Josefina, instead of throwing themselves upon Candita, held each other's hands and only stared at her.

"I'm not sick any more," Candita said. "Please talk as much as always."

Candita went to the window and looked out on their street.

Nothing had changed. After so long, it was the same. Estrellita's mother was still calling to her to come up. And Estrellita was again promising to come "in one moment, in one moment." A radio was broadcasting a ball game and another was offering a verse about Chiquita Banana. Mr. Calles, not far away, was practicing the spaghetti theme song, *La Paloma*.

The familiar good smells of the house floated in the air. Mama was cooking an *arroz con dulce*. The table was covered with a white plastic cloth and the green vase was crowded with red paper carnations.

Soon she would return to school. She would see Linda again. Perhaps Barnabe now would

131

be in another class. Rafael was already in Miss Wood's class. She was glad that she, at least, would remain with Miss Singer.

"Candita," Mama said, "if you are tired, you must sleep. Your bed is ready."

"I am not tired. Please tell me all you did while I was not here."

"We waited for your return to us," said Mama.

"This morning," Renaldo said, "while I waited for the hour to go to the hospital to bring you home, I walked a long distance. I came to a large building. Around its base there were animal forms, carved in stone. Truthfully carved. It was a language I understood."

"I would like to see those carvings, too, Renaldo," Candita said.

"I would like to show them to you before I leave. It is a language, I think, that exists everywhere. People understand each other through the work of their hands. Language is nothing compared to this."

"We shall miss you when you leave," Fernanda said. Fernanda was changed. She did not laugh at all today.

132

After a few minutes, Renaldo said, "I must walk and I must think. I will go out and I will return soon."

Fernanda stood up. "If I walk with you, will it disturb your thoughts, Renaldo?"

"No, Fernanda, I would like it if you would walk with me."

"Now it is time that you go to sleep, Candita," Mama said.

She did not refuse, but having got into bed she could not sleep. She shut her eyes and it was as if, near by but she did not know exactly where, there was an answer. There was a question for Renaldo to answer, and it was also a question for her. *What to do?*

She dressed slowly. It was early, but already the day was hot. Candita reached for her thinnest dress, a blue and white dress Mama had made for her.

Fernanda came in haste. "No, no, for your return to school we have found a more suitable dress." There, in Fernanda's hands, was a pink dress of silk, soft and light as paper. "Do you like it?"

133

"It is very beautiful."

Fernanda said, "I will walk with you, Candita. Because it is your first day at school, I will take you there."

Mama tied a ribbon in Candita's hair, and as she was doing this, Candita said, "Mama, I would like to keep the name I have. I would like to remain Candita Rivera. It would be, then, as if I still belong to you. Is it possible?"

"I think it is possible," Mama said, putting both her arms around Candita delicately, not to disturb the folds of her dress.

Jorge shot out of his door. "Take me to school, Candita. I want to go with you as always."

Jorge ran ahead. "Not so fast, Jorge," Fernanda called out. "Remember Candita is not yet strong."

Candita hardly recognized herself as she looked at her reflection in the windows of the stores. Not alone was the dress beautiful, it seemed also to make her look taller. Her hair looked smoother and more shining, it seemed to her, because of the new pink dress. Even

134

her face seemed changed, and her eyes larger.

"My teacher gave me two books," Jorge said. "These books are too hard. I will give them back to my teacher. You can read to me from your book, Candita, as before."

Jorge would have to begin to read by himself soon. Because when she was gone—it was difficult to think of going away now, while walking on Broadway as always—but when she was gone, he would have to get used to reading by himself.

Fernanda took her hand. "I have come with you because it is your first day, Candita, but there is this, too, that I must tell you now. I do not know what you will say, but I hope you will be happy. Candita, that night while we were walking, Renaldo and I—I discovered a new thing. I discovered that I am in love. Yes, truly."

Again happiness swept over Candita, as when Jeanie had said she could talk English, and when Mama had said Renaldo was coming. She was listening to Fernanda and hoping she knew what Fernanda was about to say.

135

"I am in love with Renaldo, and Renaldo loves me, too. We are going to be married, Candita."

"It is what I hoped," Candita said.

"Now we shall all go back to Mayagüez, you and Renaldo and I. We shall be together. There will be no loneliness for Renaldo. And no struggle with English for you and for me. And always beautiful weather. What do you say to that, Candita?"

"I am very happy, Fernanda."

"There will be more room here for Mama and Papa and Margarita and Josef and their little ones. And one day we shall come in a plane to visit them. I can work there, too, Candita."

Fernanda would help her to make a home for Renaldo. With Fernanda's help and having Fernanda beside her, it would be easy.

She would be where she longed to be. She would see Paquita each day, and she would look at the bright flowers and trees of Puerto Rico again. Never again would she be cold.

18

THERE was a surprise for her in the class-room.

Red and blue paper streamers decorated the room, and in the center a big swinging sign said: WELCOME BACK CANDITA

Fernanda had come upstairs with her.

"Candita," she whispered, "it is as if you

137

are the president!" Then, embarrassed to be the tallest in a crowd of children, Fernanda kissed Candita quickly and hurried away.

Everyone was there. Rafael had come downstairs from Miss Wood's class. Linda and Carmen and the boys crowded around her.

"I am glad to be back," she said. Suddenly she was talking, not Spanish as they were, but English. "Thank you for this big welcome."

"Candita talks English like Miss Singer. She is entirely changed."

"She is no longer the shy one."

"She has been in a hospital for learning English."

Everyone was laughing and talking in both languages.

She looked toward the window. Her little clay animals were still on the window sill. Everything looked the same and everything was different. The children were more talkative. Everything was better than she remembered. Everything was livelier and happier.

Then the best thing of all happened. Miss Singer came into the room carrying a white and pink cake. She held the cake so Candita could read the words written on it:

THREE CHEERS FOR CANDITA RIVERA

"The words are composed by Rafael," Miss Singer said in Spanish. "It means 'Brava! Brava! Brava! Candita.' We shall eat the cake after lunch. In the meantime it will be a decoration for my desk." Miss Singer put the cake in the center of her desk under a transparent cake cover.

"This cake is in a cage," said Rafael, "so that it cannot run away from us."

All eyes fixed themselves on the cake to see if it would attempt to run away.

Rafael stood up. Today Rafael was the most talkative of all. "Miss Singer, Candita is no longer the shy one. She does not stop talking. And do you know which language she speaks?"

"Which?" asked Miss Singer.

"English," Rafael said. "No more Spanish. This hospital makes an operation and it removes the Spanish language from Candita."

Everyone burst into laughter.

Candita laughed, too. She said, "I can still speak Spanish, but today is the day for English."

Even Miss Singer was surprised. "It sounds fine, Candita—as if you were born in New York."

It was just as she had dreamed. She said, "I have a new friend. She does not speak Spanish so I must speak English to her."

"So, Candita," said Miss Singer, "I suppose it is time for you to leave me. You will go to a class where you will learn all the things you should be learning at your age instead of English only. And Linda is going with you."

Candita looked downcast.

"We do not want to leave you, Miss Singer," Linda said.

"You will both like Miss Taney," Miss Singer said, "and this party is to celebrate Candita's return, and also her leaving us. Rafael, bring the record player to the center of the room, please."

Rafael brought the record player and also

140

did a dance he made up to the music of a
rumba, which was the first of the records. It
was a dance Rafael invented while listening to
the music. It required handstands besides the
usual rumba steps.

Carmen sang a song in Spanish and then

sang it again, translating it this time into English. She hurried all the English words together to make them come out even with the music:

"So-everything's-now-O.K."

It made everyone laugh. Carmen had to sing it over and over with the English words.

After lunch Candita cut the cake. It was a cake "of rare quality and five floors high" as Luis said. Candita said she would not eat her slice but would take it home to show to her family and to Jorge, who liked cake.

Miss Singer refused to allow this. "This half of the cake is for your family. We can only eat half here. I have saved the box so you can take the rest home." Miss Singer wrapped it carefully and tied the box with silver ribbons.

The door opened.

"Come in, Miss Taney," said Miss Singer.

They all stared at Miss Taney.

She was tall and thin and the opposite of Miss Singer, who was golden-haired and often smiled. Miss Taney did not smile. Her hair was brown and her eyeglasses had no diamonds around their rims.

Miss Singer waved at Linda and Candita, and said to Miss Taney, "These two are yours now."

Miss Taney looked seriously first at Linda and then at Candita, and said, "Well, you two will have to hurry. We're late with spelling upstairs."

Candita felt as if she were again leaving Mayagüez and the friends of her childhood.

Linda shrugged her shoulders and looked without hope at Carmen. Carmen shrugged her shoulders, too, and shook her head in sympathy.

19

THERE had been only seven in Miss Singer's class, but Room 415 was crowded. Miss Taney pointed to an empty seat. Both girls looked at it and stood undecided.

"Sit down, sit down," Miss Taney said.

Linda slipped into the seat at the back and Candita saw the other empty one. It was in front of Miss Taney's desk. The children all stopped what they were doing to watch her make her way to the front of the room.

It was again almost as it had been the first day. Miss Taney talked about yesterday's spelling homework, and the children put notebooks out on their desks. Then Miss Taney asked for arithmetic homework. Everyone, except Candita, seemed to know what to do. Miss Taney asked some arithmetic questions that seemed impossible to understand. Candita sat listening and not understanding.

Miss Taney had entirely forgotten her, and Linda, too.

"Reading," said Miss Taney suddenly. Notebooks were put away. Readers were brought out.

The girl beside Candita raised her hand. "She hasn't got a book," the girl said, and pointed at Candita.

"Yes, yes," said Miss Taney, "get her a complete set, and a set for the other one, too. Two complete sets, Maria, please."

Maria went to the cupboard and came back

with four books for Candita.

She banged them down on Candita's desk and went back for Linda's.

"Quietly," said Miss Taney sternly.

The books made everything better. Candita saw that the book on top was *Stories for Fourth Grade*. The class was reading from that book. One boy stood up and began to read aloud.

Maria leaned toward her and showed her the story they were reading.

It was easy. She could read faster than the boy who was reading aloud. When she had read ahead for a whole page, she looked at the other books in the small tower on her desk: *Arithmetic* was one, and *A History of the United States* was another, and the fourth had the title *Our Language*.

Miss Taney said, "Now, Candita, read on from paragraph two."

She had read so far ahead, she had turned to the next page. Now Maria again leaned toward her, turned back the page, and showed her the place.

"Stand up, please, Candita, and read." Miss

Taney was impatient.

Candita stood up. The words were far more difficult to say than to read. She began and stopped.

"Go on, go on, we haven't all day."

She began again. If she read a word wrong, perhaps they would all laugh at her, and Miss Taney would send her back to Miss Singer's class—that would be even worse than not coming upstairs to her own grade. She took a deep breath and in a small voice she read the words she saw. She did the very best she could.

Miss Taney twice called out, "Louder, please. No one can hear you at the back."

"Next," said Miss Taney abruptly after two paragraphs, "John."

No one had laughed.

Candita sat, and John began to read. His voice was loud and he hurried along, skipping words here and there.

"Not so loud," said Miss Taney. "Slow up. Read every word that's there, John."

When the bell rang at the end of the afternoon, Miss Taney said, "Candita, stay for a minute."

"Yes, yes," Candita said, forgetting Jorge, forgetting everything, and hoping only that Miss Taney would not send her back to Miss Singer's class to learn more English.

"Candita," Miss Taney said after everyone else had gone, "you must keep reading aloud and *please* practice talking English. I would like you, especially, to work for the speech prize. Do you know what that is?"

Candita shook her head.

"Each graduation a speech prize is given by Mrs. Peterson. It goes to someone who has come to our school speaking only Spanish and has learned to speak English so well that at graduation she or he can make a farewell speech in English. I thought today, while you were reading, that you would be the one to win the speech prize two years from now."

Candita stood staring at Miss Taney and wondering if she had understood all she had said. "Thank you, Miss Taney, I am not sure—"

"We must try—whether we are sure or not!" Miss Taney stood up. "Someday you must make us a few clay animals for our window sill, too. I asked Miss Singer about hers and she said you had made them."

"I will make all that you want," Candita said.

She wanted to tell Miss Taney she would try for the speech prize and that she would make one thousand animals if Miss Taney wanted them, that it was worth having an appendicitis operation if so many good things happened afterward. All she could say was, "Thank you, Miss Taney."

She ran downstairs. Jorge had gone. She began to hurry home.

Everything was beginning today. As if the plane had brought her only yesterday, everything was beginning all over again. Only it was much better than it had been the day she had really come. Much, much better.

When she was at the corner of their street, she saw Jorge.

"Where have you been? Were you lost?" Jorge asked.

"I have been talking to my teacher," Candita said. She wanted to tell him everything, about the prize and the graduation speech and even about being asked to make more clay animals, but it was too much. It was as bad as not having anything to say. She had so much to tell him she did not know how to begin.

"What are these books? I will carry a few," Jorge said.

She divided her books and gave him two and kept two to carry. "We will read them when we arrive home."

"Do you know more stories, Candita? I have not heard a story for a long time."

"Yes, I will read to you from these new books."

She opened the door. No one else was at home. The afternoon sunshine filled the room. The bright red of the paper flowers was reflected in the large tin frying pan that hung on the wall above the stove. A plate on the table had two deep red peaches on it.

The voices and noises of the street seemed far away. The radio in Mrs. Ranchera's apartment downstairs was turned on, but it, too, seemed far away. Candita stood for a moment looking about, happy to be here, seeing and hearing everything, looking at the big chair at the window and the smaller chair beside it.

"I will read to you first out of this book, Jorge. The name of this book is A *History of the United States.*"

She began to read aloud, slowly and carefully. "The discovery of America was an accident, the result of Europe's desire for trade with China and India. In 1492, Christopher Columbus set out under the flag of Spain in an attempt to reach the East by sailing due west across the Atlantic. Columbus failed because his way was blocked by two huge continents. . . ."

Jorge was leaning forward. He had put his elbows on his knees and his chin in his hands.

From downstairs came, "Estrellita, Estrellita!" Someone turned up Mrs. Ranchera's radio and distant music filled the air. The light in the sky began to fade, and the cooking smells, rising up the stairs and through the hallway and through the keyhole, pervaded the apartment.

Everything was right.

Jorge sat listening and Candita sat reading A *History of the United States.*

It was like *Bushy Tail*, but it was better than *Bushy Tail* because *Bushy Tail* was for little children and she was no longer a little child. It was a story, but it was better than a story because it had really happened.

There was a quick rapping at the door. "Candita, is Jorge there?"

"Jorge is here, Mrs. Torres."

Mrs. Torres burst into the room. "I am sorry I am so late."

"Is it late?" Neither she nor Jorge had looked at the clock. Neither she nor Jorge had thought about supper.

"It is six o'clock!"

Someone was running up the stairs.

Fernanda, carrying two bags of groceries, came in. Renaldo, with more groceries, followed her.

"There is a big crowd in the market," Fernanda said. "I have been standing on a line for an hour."

"And I, too," said Mrs. Torres, "and a lady with many things tries to go in front of me— I say to her, 'Do not stop here—I must hurry home—my little boy is waiting for me.' I do not speak English, so I say all this in Spanish and she answers also in Spanish—she says, 'I, too, must hurry—you are not the only one who must hurry,' and she says, 'This neighborhood has only Puerto Ricans now—it is now no longer a good neighborhood—I am myself from Havana,' and she puts her nose in the air, and I say, 'That is a very bad way to talk and anyway you must go in back of me.' So she goes in back of me and then the lady talks to me that is in front of me but as she talks in English I cannot tell you what she said to me, but I can tell you she does not look sympathetic, and it cannot be a good thing and I say nothing, for that is enough fighting for one day and—"

Mama arrived. "Candita, you must eat your supper now. You are still not strong."

Jorge said, "I don't want to go home. I want to stay here."

"Come back tomorrow," said Mama. "Now

154

we must take care of Candita. She is as thin as a pipe. A thin pipe."

"Jorge, you have not seen the candy I have bought," said Mrs. Torres.

Mama looked sternly at Mrs. Torres.

"But only when you finish your supper," said Mrs. Torres hastily, "and it is for us all. The sooner you eat your supper, the sooner we will all have this candy."

Candita was playing with the little girls. She cut paper hats from a newspaper and gave each one a hat. She drew animals for them on paper bags. They all sat on the floor while Mama fried onions. The lovely smell filled the room. Fernanda and Renaldo set the table.

She loved this time of day, Candita was thinking, when the little girls watched with admiration the things she could do.

Uneasily she remembered her decision. She was going back to Puerto Rico with Renaldo and Fernanda, but during this day that had been full of surprises, she had put it altogether out of her head.

She would have to leave the new class. She

would have to leave Jorge. She would have to tell Jorge he must begin to read by himself. She would even have to leave Mama and the big new family she had found here. And Miss Singer. And Miss Taney.

Martina and Josefina went to sleep. Candita went to bed, too. Mama and Papa, Fernanda and Margarita, Josef and Renaldo were talking together in the room beside hers. It did not seem as if there were too many people now. In Mayagüez there would be only three in their family.

Already, thinking of it, she missed the others. The sharing is bad, Pedro Chavez had said, but Pedro Chavez was wrong. There are times when it is bad, perhaps, when they are strangers who share—but the sharing is sometimes like this, she thought. She wished she could talk to Jeanie. When Jeanie talked with her, everything seemed better.

20

THERE was a letter for Candita when she came home from school. It was on the table leaning against the vase of bright red paper carnations. Never before had she received a letter of her own. In the corner of the envelope was the name *Jeanie Garnett*.

Dear Candita,

First let me thank you for giving me the beautiful cat. I shall keep it all my life.

Something else happened and it is this I am writing about. When I unwrapped your gift my father was in the room. I told him about you, Candita, and that your father had carved the little cat. My father said, "Find out if your little friend's father will drop by to see me at the museum." So that is what I am writing about. Do you think Renaldo will go to see him? I am enclosing my father's card. He suggested Wednesday at 4. He also said if Renaldo had any other little animal carvings to bring them along.

Candita, please ask him to go to see my father.

Love,

Jeanie

When at least Renaldo came, everything was different than she had expected. She had thought she would have to beg him to go. But when she said that Jeanie's father would like to see more of his work, Renaldo said, "Then I will have to borrow the rabbit from you."

Renaldo would go and who could say? Candita thought. Perhaps one day, and perhaps it would not be too far away, they would return to New York. Jeanie and Jeanie's father and she and Renaldo and Fernanda would all meet. They would talk about the work of Renaldo

158

and the work of Jeanie's father. Renaldo would make more and more carvings in the meantime. Not only of cats and rabbits but of animals of the zoo and perhaps of people, too.

Perhaps Renaldo would carve a whole set of animals while they were in Puerto Rico. When they returned, she would bring them to Miss Singer's classroom and Miss Taney's, too, and there would be enough for Jeanie, too, and for her father.

The next day Miss Taney again asked Candita to wait after school. When the others had gone, Miss Taney took a flat package from her desk.

"You remember what I said about the graduation speech, Candita? This is a book of poems. You must practice reading them aloud."

Candita held the package in both hands.

"Unwrap it, Candita." Miss Taney helped by snipping the string.

A *Child's Garden of Verses* was the name of the book. There was a picture of a child lying in a field of daisies on the cover and also the words *By Robert Louis Stevenson*.

"I hope you like it," said Miss Taney.

"I like it, Miss Taney." There was no use taking the book because she would be far away at graduation. Someone else would make the speech and would need this book. "Thank you very much, but—"

"I bought it for you, Candita. You needn't return it."

She wanted very much to read it. She could not tell Miss Taney yet about leaving. But when she had read it, she would return it. Then she would say, *I am leaving, Miss Taney. I am going back to Puerto Rico. I return this book to you now.*

"I will read it today."

"Aloud," said Miss Taney severely, but it was only outside that Miss Taney was severe. Candita had already discovered that, inside, Miss Taney was exactly like Miss Singer.

Candita went home slowly, looking into the book as she walked. While waiting at a crossing she read:

> I saw you toss the kites on high
> And blow the birds about the sky;
> And all around I heard you pass,
> Like ladies' skirts across the grass—

160

O wind, a-blowing all day long,
O wind, that sings so loud a song!

It was like music.

At home she read all the poems. She read the whole book and then read it again, just as Jorge would ask her to do. She looked away from the book and found she knew all the words of a poem she had read only twice:

How do you like to go up in a swing,
Up in the air so blue?
Oh, I do think it the pleasantest thing
Ever a child can do!

Her eyes fell on the neat pile of boxes and bags and a large suitcase. All were ready for the trip to Puerto Rico.

Jorge drummed on the door and called loudly, "Candita, open the door."

Jorge came in, two books in his hands. "I waited for you, Candita, a long time. Where were you?"

"I talked to my teacher."

"You were bad in school?"

"No, I talked to my teacher about a book."

"Here are two new books, Candita. These are the ones that are too hard."

"You like stories very much, Jorge, so you

must go to the library every day to read new stories. By yourself. When it is time for your mother to come home, you can leave the library."

"I will go if you will go with me," said Jorge.

She did not want to spoil this afternoon. Tomorrow she would surely tell Jorge. Today she read A *Child's Garden of Verses* to him until his mother came.

Fernanda arrived at the same time. "Candita, I invite you to a wedding. Can you guess whose wedding it is?"

Fernanda was beautiful today. She had made a white carnation of paper and then put it in her hair.

"Your wedding, I hope."

"Yes, mine and Renaldo's."

Fernanda drove away all Candita's unhappy thoughts. Fernanda bent to Candita and kissed her, and Candita put both arms around her.

"Look at this dress, Candita. It is for you for our wedding. I have even bought you white ribbons. See."

It was the most beautiful dress she had ever

seen. The ruffles became wider down the skirt and there was a dainty edge of lace at the neck and around the short sleeves.

"Now you will see mine," said Fernanda. "You must see my wedding dress." She was enormously proud of it. It was long and white and shining.

"And see," Fernanda said, "I almost forgot to show you the present you will bring to Paquita."

It was a ring of pale blue enamel and there was a bracelet that matched it.

Renaldo came in and put an envelope on the table. "We now have the plane tickets for us all," said Renaldo.

Candita was happy and unhappy at the same time. It made her happy to be with Fernanda and with Renaldo. It was good to think of Mayagüez and the little house of Renaldo's, and the sea and the white beach and the warm sun and Paquita. Then she thought of all those she would leave in New York—and the happiness became as the thin mist around the plane, appearing, changing, and at last disappearing.

21

THE NEXT MORNING when she called for Jorge, he answered through the door. "Go alone today. I am not going to school." Then, while walking down the street, she heard Jorge's voice calling, "Wait for me, Candita. I am coming."

She stopped and turned. Jorge's head was lowered and he was rubbing his eyes at every few steps.

"What has happened, Jorge?"

"Nothing."

"Why are you crying, then?"

"I am not crying," Jorge said, tears rolling out of his eyes. Candita dried his eyes with her handkerchief. "Tell me, Jorge."

"No more going to school with you. No more reading."

"What has happened?"

"We are moving. My father has lost his job again. There is not too much work in the factory for my mother. We cannot pay this rent, so we are going to move. We will live with my aunt and the rent will be cheap, for we will share everything. My mother does not like this aunt and there is always fighting when they are together, and I do not like this aunt, too."

"Where does your aunt live?"

"Far away. Two blocks away. My uncle works on a delivery truck. Sometimes he takes Filipe along. Filipe is my cousin. He is five years old."

"We will be moving, too, Jorge."

"You cannot pay the rent, too? Maybe you will move together with us." Jorge looked hopefully at Candita.

"Fernanda, Renaldo, and I are going back to Puerto Rico."

166

He stood still. Then he began to cry harder.

"I think you will like your new house," Candita said, "for you will have Filipe. You can go with Filipe to the library. You can take home all the books you want from the library. You can read to Filipe."

"I can read better than Filipe. My father says when he gets a job he will buy a television set. Will you come back, Candita?"

"I think I will come back one day."

"When you come back, will you come to see me?"

"Yes, yes, Jorge. I will come. Write your new address on a paper for me. I will write you a letter from Puerto Rico."

He stopped crying. Together they ran all the rest of the way to school.

Perhaps it was best to say good-by at the end of the day today as if she were going home for the afternoon. When she returned to Mayagüez, she would send Miss Taney a post card with a view of Puerto Rico. It would explain everything.

Candita walked to the door of the room and

turned to Miss Taney. "Now I am leaving, Miss Taney. Good-by."

"Good afternoon," Miss Taney said, not looking up and writing in her book. Then she looked up. "I nearly forgot. Candita, we have always had a party in our room on the last day of the term. You remember you promised to make me some little clay animals for decorations? I bought the clay for them—"

Now. Now would be the time to tell Miss Taney she would never see her again. Now was the time to say there would be no days left in which to make the little clay animals.

No, not now. Better to write the post card.

"—but I've locked the closet door, Candita, so tomorrow be sure to take the clay home."

Tomorrow she would no longer be here. She walked downstairs slowly. Jorge was sitting on the school steps.

"Let us go to the library together," she said. "You are beginning to read better each day."

"I don't want to go to the library," Jorge said. "I want to go home. To your house. My teacher gave me this book. This is a book you will have to read to me. It is a hard book."

168

Suddenly she thought of another place to take Jorge. "Would you like to see a museum?"

She had learned the address from the card Jeanie had sent. Today was Wednesday, the day Renaldo was going to the museum to see Jeanie's father. They would meet Renaldo and they would walk home together, and Renaldo would tell her if they would come back someday when he had carved more animals.

"What's a museum?"

"I will show you one."

This time Jorge stopped at only one shop window, where a cardboard man regularly raised and lowered a razor to a soapy chin.

It was a long walk.

"Let's see what's inside," Jorge said, looking at the huge museum building. "If they have a bench, I will sit down. I am tired."

The history of all living things was here, Jeanie had said.

"It is like the history book I read to you," Candita said, but it was entirely different.

There were wide marble corridors and great arched openings. It was dim and quiet. It was as though they had walked into a strange, distant country. Into many strange, distant countries. Once Papa had said, "There are not too many quiet places in New York," but here it was quiet.

Candita and Jorge stood still. On either side of the wide hall there were tall glass walls. Beyond these were forests in sunlight, animals and birds gathered at water holes or standing in secret clearings in thick forests.

"It is a little like Mayagüez," whispered Candita to Jorge, who could not remember Puerto Rico. "In Puerto Rico, there are trees like these."

The most curious were the animals. These stood or lay or seemed to graze in the green lands behind the clear glass. The most graceful and magnificent animals were here, having the strangest and most musical names: *eland* and *springbok*, she read, and *tahr*. Leaping animals and great brilliant birds.

They were so real Jorge said about each one, "That one is alive, no?"

Jorge held Candita's hand tightly. For the first five minutes. Then he began to dart about into the shadows of the great halls, running back to her after his short trips. Jorge was as anxious to have Candita read the descriptions on each exhibit as he had been to hear her read from a book. He forgot he was tired.

"Look at this one," he said. "Candita, here is one I would like to take a ride on. This place is O.K. This place is the best place in the world."

She wanted to look at the animals until she knew every one of them. She wanted to make clay figures of them. It was as if here were a hallful of friends.

Some of these trees and plants she had seen, but others were new. She looked at them until she could close her eyes and still see them all clearly.

It seemed to them they had been there only a few minutes when a gong sounded. Someone called out, "Closing time!"

In the main hall the clock said five.

Jorge's mother would be looking for him, and Mama, too, would worry over them.

22

THEY tried to run, but after half a block, Jorge stopped.

"I am tired," he said, standing still. "Remember the horses with the stripes? Did you see the horses with the stripes?"

"Zebras," said Candita. "That is their name."

"I would like a ride on one. And I would like to see them run. I would like to see the striped horses running."

172

"You will have to go to Africa for that," said Candita. "It said they live in Africa. Come on, Jorge."

"Then I will go there," said Jorge, beginning to walk again. "I will go to see all the striped horses. Where is Africa?"

"Far away. Hurry, we will be late," Candita said. But she, too, could not walk any faster. Suddenly she remembered Renaldo.

He, too, would have seen the animals. She was glad she had seen them. When she and Renaldo were far away from New York, they would remember the animals and talk of them.

She began to walk more and more slowly.

"Hurry," said Jorge, looking at her. "We are late."

Now, besides the school, she was thinking, there was the museum. Now that she had discovered this magic place, she would have to leave it, too, together with Miss Taney and Jeanie and Jorge and Mama and all the others.

Everyone was at home, even Mr. and Mrs. Torres and Jorge's grandmother.

She expected Mama to say, We thought

you were both lost. We were going to the police station. Instead Mama said, "Candita is here, too, now, with Jorge."

It was as if they had been speaking of something entirely different.

Mrs. Torres was scolding Jorge. "Where have you been?" she said, not waiting for him to answer. "I have so much work and you are late and you know we must begin to pack if we are to move—so good-by," Mrs. Torres said, turning to the others. "Good-by. Tell me tomorrow what you have decided."

Candita looked at her family. As she had come upstairs, she had heard their raised voices in conversation. As if they were hiding something from her, the conversation had now stopped. And as if Mama wished to change the subject, she said, "It is late. Let us all have our supper at once. Candita, here are the plates." She began handing the plates from the cupboard to Candita.

Margarita took the children by the hand, and brought them to the table. "Let the children eat first. We can have supper later, and

174

them, for Renaldo had said "fifty-five dollars each week." It sounded like much. There would surely be enough so that Renaldo could buy clay and wood for himself, and perhaps a little for her until she could earn some money herself.

With Renaldo's help she would begin to model animals and people. One day she would make the figures of Jorge and Alberto as she had seen them wrestling in front of the school that long ago afternoon.

23

IT WAS an exceptional wedding. In the golden and rose light of the stained-glass windows, Fernanda and Renaldo looked serious and happy. The perfume of the true white carnations filled the church.

Everyone had come from the house they lived in. Even old Mrs. Ranchera.

"Whatever happens is for the best," said Mrs. Ranchera. "Fernanda is very lucky and beautiful, too. Especially it is lucky that the day is fine. That is a very good sign. It is a sign she is not greedy, nor is Renaldo greedy. No one can say that one or the other has scraped the bottom of the pot, as is said when it rains. When the day is fine, everything is for the best."

Mr. and Mrs. Torres each held one of Jorge's hands.

Afterward it was as if their small apartment had obligingly stretched its walls to make room for neighbors and friends. Everyone could, by trying, fit into it. All the guests moved slowly and admiringly about the table. The good things were piled high. There were true white carnations on either side of an enormous tower of a wedding cake.

Jorge detached himself from his parents and stood beside Candita.

"Remember the animals?" he said, as if she were in danger of forgetting him since so much else was happening. "Candita, will you take me to that place again?"

"Yes, yes, Jorge, soon. We will meet as al-

181

ways and walk to school and from school, too. As always. And go to see the animals in the museum."

Mama was making a speech. "To the fortunate ones," she said, "we wish happiness and wealth. To Renaldo and Fernanda and Candita. They have always been in our family and there is no change. They are still our family."

"*Salud, pesetas, y tiempo para gozarlas,*" said Paco Torres. He then explained in English for those that might not understand: "This means, good health and money, and the time to enjoy the money and the good health."

Papa came to Fernanda and to Renaldo and to Candita and shook hands with them as if they had newly met, as if he were someone entirely different from Papa.

"We shall soon go with you to find an apartment of your own," said Papa. He turned to Mama. They both laughed. "The truth is we do not want you to live too far away." Again Mama and Papa laughed, and Margarita and Josef, too.

182

"Do not keep it from them any longer," said Mama.

"Renaldo and Fernanda and Candita are now our neighbors," announced Papa. "We have made the necessary arrangements. As Mr. and Mrs. Torres have decided to move away from this house, we inquired about their apartment for Renaldo and Fernanda and Candita. As you will see, they are now our neighbors. It is only a matter of a single door away."

"I know this place," Jorge said. "I can come here in five minutes."

"Yes, yes," said Candita. "You must come as always. It is as if it is still yours."

"Let us see this apartment of Fernanda's and Renaldo's," someone said.

Papa held up a key. "This is now yours, Renaldo. For your own house."

Renaldo unlocked the door.

There were new white curtains at the window. In the center of the new table there was a long white narrow box.

Fernanda and Candita untied the white rib-

183

bons around the box. The scent was like the perfume of the flowers and bushes of Maya-güez at nightfall.

"For the Montez family," the card read. "With love from Anna L. Peterson."

Under the window in the smaller of the two small rooms was Candita's bed. She stood beside it and looked out.

Getting up in the morning, she would see from here a center island on Broadway. There were trees and bushes growing there. She would see a little piece of blue sky, too. Trees and bushes below, and blue sky overhead. With the perfume of Mrs. Peterson's flowers filling the little room, it was like a corner of Mayagüez. A corner of Mayagüez—and also New York. New York—and also a corner of Mayagüez.

F
LEW
LEWITON, MINA
Candita's choice

DATE DUE			
APR 27			
NOV 15			
NOV 29			
FEB 5			
JAN 16			
JAN 23			
FEB 25			
DEC 2			
			ALESCO